Love UNCOVERED

AMAZON BESTSELLING AUTHOR

LAURA BARNARD

Suzanne

Really hope you enjoy!

Love + Laughs

Laura Barnard

x x x

First Edition

A CIP catalogue record for this title is available from the British Library.

Dedication

This book is dedicated to my Auntie Mad, one of my biggest cheerleaders. Thank you so much for everything you do for us.

Chapter 1

Friday 21st July

'You need to calm your cooch,' Erica says before following with a maniacal laugh.

I smile to myself then grab my crotch jokingly. 'I can't help it that she's excited.'

After a whole month of living with her and Jack, listening to them shag non-stop, I'm finally getting Tom down to Brighton.

I haven't been able to get him out of my head since that holiday to Luna Island just over a month ago. Those big broad shoulders, blonde hair and piercing green eyes. We had an instant connection and spent most of the holiday fucking like animals.

And I can't wait to get my greedy little hands on him.

Have I heard from him since we got back from holiday? No, of course not. Guys like Tom don't text or call, they just show up and demand sex with their very presence. And I can't fucking wait.

Don't get me wrong, I've carried on having sex, you know, just to de-stress, but after shagging him all holiday it's like I know nothing will live up to him. He's a fucking beast in bed!

'All I'm saying,' Erica warns with a cautionary smile, 'is not to jump up at him, fanny first, as soon as he arrives.'

'I'll try,' I joke, rolling my eyes.

All the guys are coming down for a weekend in Brighton: Tom, Nicholas and Charlie. I'm guessing it's the highlight of their month. Brighton is a fucking gem. I can't imagine the boredom of living somewhere normal like Peterborough. I shudder at the thought.

'Well, get ready. They'll be arriving at their hotel in the next two hours.'

Butterflies dance in my stomach. I grin and waggle my eyebrows comically.

'I'll be ready, don't worry.'

But the truth is that I'm nervous. Why the fuck I am, I'm not sure. I never get worried. Men are the one thing I know I can handle. They're ruled by their dicks so if you flash a bit of boob they're putty in your hands.

But something about seeing Tom again has me fidgeting with my necklace and feeling like I'm back in high school.

The thing is that there's no promise Tom is even looking forward to seeing me. He could be excited for all the potential Brighton pussy on offer.

'Are you nervous?' Alice asks me, a bewildered smile on her bright-red painted lips.

'No! You're nervous!' I retort like a child.

She grins big, widening her sea green eyes. 'Okay, Brooke, whatever you say.'

Dammit, that bitch has always been able to read me.

'I don't know why we're bothering to meet up with his mates,' Evelyn whines. 'We already have to put up with Jack full time.'

That girl seriously needs to get laid. It might dislodge the stick out of her arse.

Two hours later and we're meeting them outside their hotel. I spot him before he sees me. Tom 'Manwhore' Maddens. God, he's as hot as ever in dark jeans and a white shirt, his broad shoulders barely fitting in it. They deffo put something in the water up there in Peterborough.

He spots me and grins, a cheeky glint in his eyes.

'Well, well, well,' he says, his piercing green eyes dancing with mischief, 'look who got hotter.'

'Moi?' I flutter my eyelashes, faking shyness. I offer

him my hand for him to kiss, but he instead uses it to pull me hard into his solid chest.

I look up at his face, my chest heaving from the shock and proximity of those lips. The urge to reach out and touch them is strong. Or, you know, to sit on his face.

'You look utterly fuckable,' he says with a smirk.

Jesus, why is it he makes me so hot and irrational? I'm sweating like this is a first date in high school.

'You're not looking too bad yourself,' I retort, licking my lips.

He leans over so his mouth is down to my ear, lowering his voice to a whisper. 'You should see how pretty my hotel room is.'

I pull back, my heart rate beating so loudly I'm surprised he can't hear it.

'Play your cards right and you never know.'

Well, I want to keep *some* bloody mystery. Not give him confirmation that he's getting a bunk up later, when, well... okay he totally is. I want me some more 'Manwhore' Maddens. But I don't want him to know I'm a sure thing.

I nod around at the others in hello, but my full attention is on Tom. It's like my body craves him.

We order drinks and find our reserved booth in our local night club, Phoenix. The guys seem to be impressed with the place. It makes me wonder if there isn't anything half decent in Peterborough. I've never been there, so I'd have no idea.

I suppose when I think back to when I first arrived here I was amazed at how cool it was. Over the years I must have got pretty jaded.

I decide after a few hours of chatting loudly over the music to take the girls onto the dance floor. We need to show the guys we're not going to dote on them the whole time they're here. They're not celebrities for God's sake.

Some banging tunes come on meaning we're out there for quite some time. Next time I check my diamante watch I see that we've let forty-five minutes go past. Whoops.

I should get a drink. And, you know, check to see how Tom is. He'll probably be gagging for it, me having left him for so long. The thought makes me feel powerful.

I make my way back to our booth but there's no sign of him.

'Where's Tom?' I ask Charlie.

He avoids eye contact. 'Err... I... I don't know.'

Right... Well that's suspicious. Whatever though. I need to apply some more lipstick, anyway. Maybe buy a few more condoms while I'm there. You can't trust dudes to be prepared these days. Luckily, I'm like a girl scout with that shit.

I skip the long line of the ladies and instead go in the

nearer disabled loos. No one with disabilities ever comes here. The place is a death trap, steps almost everywhere you walk. I've no idea why they even bothered with it, but I suppose they have to. Would make more sense for them to have made it all wheelchair friendly instead.

I swing the door open, only for my eyes to be assaulted by the sight of a bare arse, pounding into some redhead who's screaming like she's being murdered. Wowzas.

'Shit, sorry!' I cry, about to turn around.

I put my hand up in front of me to protect my eyes. Only at that exact moment the guy turns his head, noticing he's been caught with his pants down. Familiar piercing green eyes meet mine.

My mouth drops open. It's Tom.

My Tom.

Fucking some random redhead in the disabled toilets. What the fuck? He's supposed to be here to see me, not shag the first thing he claps his eyes on.

He has the audacity to smile. Actually smile. 'Hey, Brooke. Wanna join in?'

I can't move. I don't think I've ever been this stunned before. Eventually, I turn around and walk numbly away, my legs as heavy as lead.

As the door slams shut behind me I hear him continue to pound into her, that bitch's screams echoing around the toilet walls.

'Brooke.' I look up, but instead of Tom rushing to catch me it's Nicholas, their heavily tattooed friend, leaning against the wall. 'You okay?'

I can't help but snort sarcastically. *Yeah, best night of my life.* Then I quickly remember myself. I don't want it getting back to Tom that I'm upset.

'Of course, I'm okay,' I shrug, straightening myself up. 'Why wouldn't I be?'

He stands up straight, his midnight blue eyes piercing me into place. 'He's not good enough for you.'

My heart rate accelerates. Did he really just say that?

Then just like that he turns and walks away. What the fuck?

I pop in to see my nan in her care home the next morning. I like to try to see her at least twice a week. She's got a chest infection right now so I'm scared she's on her last legs. With her asthma, it's always possible. It doesn't help that the woman has smoked forty a day for the last fifty years.

'Hey, Nan,' I smile, attempting not to look worried as I take in her frail frame coughing with such ferociousness it looks like she could break. 'How are you feeling?'

'Awful, my love,' she finally croaks before giving me a brave smile. 'I fear I'm on my last legs.'

I hate when she talks like this. Like she's going to die any minute. It makes me feel sick to my stomach at the thought of losing her.

'You'll be fine, Nan,' I say with an eye roll. 'You're on antibiotics. You'll be right as rain in no time.'

She takes my hand, giving it what I'm sure she thinks is a strong squeeze.

'I do worry about you,' she says, fear in her eyes.

I frown. 'You worry, about *me*? Why the hell would you worry about me? I'm not the one coughing up a lung.'

She sighs heavily. 'Because I don't want to leave this world until I know you have a man in your life to look after you.'

God, if she only knew the sad state of affairs when it came to the quality of men out there. Even ones you like, end up shagging randoms in the toilets.

'This isn't the nineteen-fifties, Nan. I don't need a man to look after me.'

She smiles sadly as if I'm missing the whole point of life. You see, my nan was happily married to my grandad until he passed away eleven years ago. She misses him every day and assumes that everyone is after the same thing. Well, not me.

I've watched as my own mother went from disastrous relationship to disastrous relationship. No thank you, I don't want that. Relationships make you stupid, vulnerable. I'd much rather keep the independence I've carved out for myself thank you very much.

'You need a good man in your life,' she insists, pity in her eyes.

I know what she's getting at. She thinks that because I grew up without my dad, there's something wrong with me. Some kind of hidden daddy issues. She's always banged on that a girl should know who her father is.

I mean, have I wondered what he's like? Of course, I have. But it's not like I'm ever going to meet him, so what's the point in torturing myself?

'I keep telling you, I'm fine.'

She shakes her head. 'Just don't get to my age and have regrets, sweetheart. If you want to do something, just take the risk and do it.'

Easier said than done. Looking for a good guy in this day and age is like looking for a slut in a convent.

I have always wondered about my dad though. I mean, growing up not knowing anything about him was weird and unsettling, yes. And it has crossed my mind more than once that I could be related to a guy I get with for all I know, which creeps me out no end. But I haven't needed a dad. I got my stability from my nan and grandad.

But she is right. What if she were to pass? Who would I have then? I definitely couldn't rely on mum or my ugly half-sisters Anastasia and Drizzela (it's actually Avery and Madison, but I prefer to call them after the ugly stepsisters in Cinderella). To put it mildly, they're vile.

Mum could only ever give a shit about herself or the guy she was dating and the other two spent their time tormenting me. I couldn't wait to get out of there and studying hard to get to Brighton Uni was my escape. I've never looked back.

But what if finding my dad opened a whole can of worms? I really don't have time for drama in my life. Right now, I'm busy enough with my friends, social life and business. I work as a freelance graphic designer and I've just got a six-month contract in-house that I really can't afford to fuck up.

Yet it does niggle at me. Oh, fuck it. I need to know who I am. Where I come from. And maybe I'll be like him. God knows, I'm nothing like my mother with her blonde hair and green eyes. Yes, I'm going to do it. I'm going to find him.

Love UNCOVERED

I just hope he wants to be found.

Chapter 2

Monday 24th July

I still can't believe how ridiculously excited I was over that manwhore Tom coming down to Brighton. What kind of self-respecting twenty-six-year-old am I? Acting like a teenager pining over one guy. That's not me. I'm a hit 'em and quit 'em kind of girl.

Still, I can't lie and say it doesn't sting when a guy doesn't want you.

My phone dings in my pocket at work. They've given me my own desk so I can get the majority of my work done here. I learnt quickly that the design director prefers to keep an eye on me.

I reach for my phone. It's probably Erica reminding me to call for milk on the way home. That woman is like my very own wife. You'd think she'd get Jack to pick up some shit once in a while—including his boxer shorts from the bathroom floor. Ew!

But instead of Erica's name it's an unknown number on screen. I frown, wondering which guy I've drunkenly given my phone number to. I did get trashed the other night after fleeing the club. It's not like I was going to stick around and catch up with Tom after he shagged some slag. So, I grabbed Alice and went to another club and got shit-faced. God knows who I gave it out to. My beer goggles can be very deceptive.

I open it up, bracing myself for a gross booty call.

Hi Brooke. Just checking you're okay?

A concerned booty call. Well this is weird. I was half expecting an unsolicited dick pic. I've had my fair share of them over the years.

Sorry, who is this? I text back. I have zero time for subtlety.

Then I drum my fingers on the table, impatiently waiting.

It's Nicholas.

Nicholas?! Shit. Nicholas is texting me? And he wants to check to see if I'm okay? What the hell? I snort to myself. He must have a thing for damsels in distress.

I wonder if Tom is with him and asking him to text. Find out if he's fucked it up with me for good. I need to play it super breezy lemon squeezy.

Yeah, I'm cool. You?

I'm fine. Just wanted to check you were okay after the whole Tom thing.

God, why is he being so nice? He barely said two words to me the whole week in Luna Island. But I suppose I was too busy obsessing over Tom to notice him.

Yeah, no biggie. He's a whore. I knew that.

There's no reply this time. God, he's weird. I put down the phone and carry on working. After a ridiculously long time another message comes through.

You deserve better than him.

I stare at my phone in shock. What the hell is going on?

I deserve better than him? I mean, yeah, duh, but why is he telling me this? It's not like I was expecting a relationship with Tom. I don't want a relationship. Not with Tom or anyone. So, Nicholas really needn't worry.

Saturday 29th July

That very next Saturday morning I'm up by 7am and planning how I'm going to find my dad.

I know that Nan never met him so that's a dead end. The only person who'll have any information at all is Mum and I really, really don't want to ask her. But needs must.

So that's how I find myself driving to Castledean at

8:30 am. God, I hope the ugly half-sisters aren't in. I could do without having to deal with them too.

As I pull into the grime-ridden council estate I grew up in, only a thirty-minute drive away. a feeling of despair settles over me. I used to feel so helpless and hopeless here. I hate reminding myself of that.

After parking up, I use my key to go in. Mum's passed out on the sofa in her dressing gown, with two empty bottles of wine beside her and a half-eaten Chinese takeaway. Just another Friday night for Mum.

I start clearing the food away, clinking the bottles together deliberately to try to rouse her. She snorts, drool hanging from her mouth. God, waking the beast is hard work.

'Time to wake up, Mother,' I snarl slapping her hard on her cheeks. I know she'll hardly feel it.

She eventually stirs, opening one eye and then the other. 'Brooke,' she utters in shock. 'What are you doing here?'

I force a smile. 'I came to see you, obviously.'

She straightens herself up on the sofa, wiping the dribble from her chin. 'Well, don't make out you come to see me every week. I haven't seen you for months.'

Haven't I been bloody lucky. It's not like she bothers calling me to check I'm not dead.

'Yeah, well I thought I'd come and check how you

are.'

She rolls her eyes. 'Always worrying about me, Brooke. I've told you to stop worrying and start being more concerned about yourself. You need to find a boyfriend.'

Ugh, my mother, ladies and gentlemen. I worry because the woman's a functioning alcoholic, but what does she worry about? Me getting a man. Because apparently that's her solution to everything. It's how she's got three kids from three different fathers and had many more boyfriends in between.

'I'm fine,' I insist through gritted teeth. 'You're the one drowning your sorrows every night.'

'I'm not drowning anything,' she snaps, curling her lip up in irritation. 'I'm just enjoying my life. You should try it sometime.'

Ugh, why does she always make out that just because I don't regularly get so shit-faced I can't talk, I'm not enjoying my life? We used to call it drinking herself mute in our family. Not that it's much of a family.

Footsteps bound down the stairs. Oh no, we woke the beasts up. Avery's the first to come into the room. She might be the youngest at only twenty-three, but she has bags under her eyes the size of Canada which make her look a lot older.

'Ugh, I guessed it would be you,' she utters with a

grunt. 'Only you would be up at this ungodly hour on a Saturday.'

I look at my watch. 'It's not even that early. But hi, Avery. Good to see you too,' I snarl sarcastically.

She grumbles back.

Madison stomps down the stairs next, a sleep mask pulled up over her ratty blonde hair.

'Jesus, Brooke! Why the fuck do you insist on trying to ruin my life? We're not all losers like you. Some of us went out and have social lives.'

I grind my teeth, my jaw already aching from the effort. 'I have a social life, thank you very much.'

She snorts as if that's ridiculous. This is what I hate. Every time I'm around them I'm made to feel like the nerdy older sister they envisage. You see, when I was younger I was a lot quieter and was in my room a lot. I wanted more than the life on the council estate and I knew the only way out would be to go to university and that's why I studied so hard. It worked when I got my place at Brighton university and got away from this dump.

'Anyway,' I look towards Mum who's moved to the kitchen to brew some coffee. I walk in and attempt to lean casually against the worktop. I'm sure normal people feel at home in their family house. 'So, I was wondering...'

She briefly looks at me while pouring her coffee. God, how am I going to bring this up without her knowing I want to meet him?

I get my pocket mirror out and pretend to look at myself.

Scrunching my face up I declare, 'I hate my nose. Do you think I got my nose from my dad?'

'Don't be ridiculous,' she snorts. 'You've got a beautiful nose.'

Ah, just when I think she'll never say anything nice about me.

'It's your ears I'd worry about.'

There she is. And dodging the question, clever bitch.

'But do you think it's like my dad's? Do you think I look like him?'

She stares at me, her arms now crossed over her chest. 'Why the sudden interest in your dad?'

She must be joking. I've always asked questions about him. She's just always dodged them.

'Why always evading the questions?' I retort.

She ignores me as if putting milk in her coffee takes great concentration.

I sigh heavily, sick of the pussyfooting around. 'Look, I want to know what my dad looks like. Is that really so bad?'

She exhales loudly, sipping from her coffee cup. 'It just hurts to think of him.'

I nearly fall over in shock. Wow, that's surprised me. Don't get me wrong, I always had the feeling that my dad was the one that got away. The one she was always looking for in all the men that followed, but she's never blatantly admitted it.

'I'll find you a picture.'

I smile gratefully. 'A name wouldn't go amiss too.'

She stares back sternly. Clearly, I pushed too quickly. 'Some things are better left in the past, Brooke.'

What the hell does she mean by that?

I end up driving back home without a photo. She said she'd dig it out for me soon. I'm not holding my breath.

When I pull up outside our flat, I spot Nicholas leaning against his car. What the hell is he doing here? Is he here to see me? No, of course he's not. Why on earth did I even think that?

I get out of the car carefully, suddenly feeling self-conscious. Do I look hot today? I didn't even put on much make-up before I left. Just some mascara and lip gloss. I was just seeing my mum after all. God, what is it about him that makes me nervous?

He smiles at me. I say smile, it's more like a smirk. Like he knows what I'm thinking. Like he knows how uncomfortable he makes me.

'Hi,' I say with a gulp. 'What are you doing here?'

'Jack's car's broken down. They didn't know when you'd be back so I came down to get him.'

He travelled all the way from Peterborough? I look at my phone, still on silent, to see four missed calls.

'Wow, you did that?'

'Yep,' he nods seriously, his eyes holding some kind of emotion I can't put my finger on. 'Otherwise he wouldn't get to see Esme this weekend.'

My womb just exploded. Esme is Jack's four-year-old daughter from a previous relationship. God, with all his tattoos it's easy to disregard how sweet Nicholas obviously is.

'Ah, you big softie,' I tease, punching him lightly on the shoulder. My God, there's a lot of lean muscle under there. Who knew?

I miss seeing them all constantly topless like on holiday. Not that I paid much attention to him then. I was always more interested in Tom—the disabled toilets shagger.

'Yeah, well I might miss him too,' he admits, arms still crossed over his chest.

'I know the feeling,' I confess. 'Since he's moved in,

I feel like I haven't had one conversation with Erica that didn't involve one of us picking up milk.'

I look over his tattoos, trying to work out what they are.

'Do you have any?' he asks, startling me. Busted.

'Sorry?'

'Tattoos,' he says, with amusement in his eyes. 'Do you have any tattoos?'

'Nope. I don't usually like them.'

'Usually?' he repeats, his penetrative stare making me breathless. 'But you like mine?' His mouth quirks up slightly at the corners. I think that's his version of a smile.

'Maybe,' I shrug non-committal. 'They suit you.'

The door opens and Jack comes out with his bags and a depressed looking Erica.

I roll my eyes. 'Jesus, Erica, he will only be gone for a weekend. He's not going off to war.'

My phone dings with a text. It's from Tom.

Hey, Sexpot. In London tonight for a conference. Fancy a bunk up?

God, he's romantic. *Not.*

But do I fancy shagging the night away, forgetting the horror that was today? Of course.

You deserve so much better.

I can't help but hear Nicholas' words repeated back

to me. He's watching me too, as if he can read my thoughts. I mean, he's right. But I'm feeling vulnerable right now. I don't fancy going out on the pull. Knowing I'm going to have good sex with a guy I already know feels like a lot less hassle right now.

I text back.

Give me the address.

He replies almost instantly.

9pm, West Croke hotel. Wear something hot.

I snort to myself. Wear something hot. Does he even know who he's talking to? Of course, I'll be wearing something hot.

Chapter 3

Saturday 29th July Continued

I'm ready to get some action. I saunter into the hotel at 9:05 pm, wanting to be fashionably late. As promised, he's waiting for me in the reception. He must have just finished some sort of dinner and dance as he's wearing a tux. Shit, he looks hot. Just like a bigger, broader, 007.

'Hey, babe,' he says giving me a glorious smile. I can't help it. I swoon.

'Hey yourself,' I retort with what I hope is a sexy grin.

'So, you ready?' he asks, his eyes lit up with mischief.

'For anything,' I smile, really hoping he doesn't want it up the arse. Even I have hard limits.

His huge hand engulfs mine. 'Come on then.'

My heart stutters. God, I need this one last fuck to get him out of my system. The stress I've been feeling needs an out, and in this instant, I'm going to get it royally fucked out of me.

He starts leading me away, but it's only when it's too late that I realise he's walking me further into the hotel rather than towards the lift. Where is he taking me? Does he want to do something kinky in public?

He escorts me into a room. I look around to see everyone is in tuxedos or evening gowns and are sat around tables. Wait, he wants me to go to the dinner and dance?

'Why are we coming in here?' I ask, trying to pull my hand away from his.

'I want to show you off,' he explains vaguely, keeping a firm grip on my hand.

He leads me to a table before I have a chance to run away.

'Everyone, this is Brooke.'

Stuffy faced people in their sixties gaze up at me, unamused. The women quickly plaster on fake as plastic smiles. It's only when I look around to take them in that I realise Nicholas is also sat at the table. Jesus how much driving has he done today?

'What are you doing here?' I can't help but ask. God, why do I sound put out by it? Way to sound friendly, Brooke.

Nicholas locks his eyes with mine. It makes me tingle down my spine, all the way to my toes. What is it about him lately? His eyes are dark and almost menacing. I tear myself away from his intense stare and look back to Tom.

'Nic works in our IT department,' Tom explains.

An older man from the table jumps up, with his hand held out. 'Lovely to meet you, Brooke.' I smile and shake his hand politely. 'May I take your coat?'

He *cannot* remove my coat. Expose to everyone my fucking Babydoll underneath? Hardly the kind of thing to be wearing to a posh do like this.

'No, thank you. I'm a bit chilly.' I fake a shiver, trying to be convincing.

As I attempt to sit down the man is laughing like I've told a joke and is attempting to help me out of my coat.

'No, honestly. I'd rather keep it on.' Oh my God, I'm sweaty. Please, please, *please,* let him just leave me alone.

'But it's so hot in here. You must be stifling in that coat.'

Jesus, man, it's only a mac. Everyone knows you only ever wear macs when you're about to flash someone.

'No, I'm honestly fine. But thank you,' I insist firmly, forcing a tight smile.

'I'm afraid that I must insist. I once had a young lady pass out on me.' He manages to take hold of my collar and pulls. The traitorous popper buttons snap open and then it's whipped off my arms.

I close my eyes in dread, knowing this will be awful. Possibly the worst thing that's ever happened to me. A collective gasp fills the room. I open one eye to see them staring back at me in horror.

Tom's eyes have widened to twice the size. He bursts out laughing, clutching his stomach like it's the funniest thing in the world.

The Babydoll is black with bondage styled straps over my breasts. It couldn't be more whorish. I have no idea what to do, so I just sit down, eager to at least hide my legs.

'Well,' Tom laughs. 'I've heard of skimpy dresses, but that really is taking the piss.'

Oh God, why is he being such a dick and embarrassing me further? I'd pick up my coat and run out of here if I was sure it wouldn't draw more attention to me. No doubt it will. I appear frozen anyway.

'Really? It's the latest in Babydoll chic,' I say, attempting to brash it out. 'Everyone in Milan is wearing them. The UK is always a little late to adjust.' I smile as confidently as I can, attempting to resist wiping the sweat currently trickling down my neck.

I feel a hand on my shoulder and look up in dread, expecting a staff member to be politely asking me to leave. It's not the type of place to rent rooms by the hour.

Instead it's Nicholas looking down at me with pity. Before I register what he's doing, he's slipped his suit jacket over my shoulders. I look up at him in shock. He's trying to help me. Wow. Talk about knight in shining armour. I must have been right about his damsel in distress fantasy.

I slip my arms into the jacket, smiling back at him with appreciation.

'Well,' the old man says, clapping his hands together as if to move on from this. 'You've missed dinner, Brooke, but here comes dessert.'

Tom leans over to whisper in my ear. 'I'm pretty sure you're my dessert. And I plan on eating you all up.'

I still can't believe I sat through a dinner in just my Babydoll. And more shocking than that, is how lovely the people treated me. I mean, I seriously doubt they didn't notice what I was wearing, but they were polite enough to try to ignore it and carry on. Very British of them.

Tom finally says the words I've been wanting to hear all night. 'Let's go to bed.'

I smile back at him, but can't help but look back at Nicholas. He's been eyeing me intensely all night making me physically squirm.

Why is it I feel he's judging me? Probably because

he warned me off Tom and yet here I am, back for more. A glutton for punishment.

I force myself to look away from him and instead follow Tom out of the room. The whole time I feel Nicholas' eyes burning into my back.

What the hell is that guy's problem with me?

Sunday 30th July

I wake up surrounded by heat. Tom's body is slumped against me, his arm slung over my chest. I roll my eyes before pushing him off. He rolls away, snoring louder but not waking.

Last night wasn't exactly what I'd anticipated. I was expecting the same sex we had on holiday, but it was different. I can't exactly put my finger on it, but it just was. I wasn't as hot for him and I hate to admit that my mind kept wandering to Nicholas and whether he thought me a slag.

Plus knowing full well that if I hadn't come tonight, Tom would have happily found another pussy to sink his dick into; well, it's off-putting. Sex with him was good—of course it was—but my heart just wasn't in it. I think I'm still pissed at him for the skank in the toilets. That or I'm actually growing up and realising I want a bit of respect.

I quickly dress, being quiet enough so as not to wake

him. I really don't fancy a chat with the guy. He's not known for his conversational skills.

I open the door still holding my shoes, the coat wrapped firmly around me. As I shut it Nicholas walks down the corridor.

Shit, just what I need. Him here judging me.

'Hey,' he nods, hands in his pockets, stopping in front of me. He leans back on one leg against the wall.

God, he looks edible in just a black t-shirt and dark denim jeans. Since when did I find this type of guy hot? I normally hate tattoos and he has them all the way up to his chin.

'Hi,' I mumble, shyly. I hate bumping into anyone doing the walk of shame. I never look my best and I like to have a face full of make up if I'm going to be judged.

'So, you did it then?' he asks, eyebrows raised.

I sigh, too tired to lie. Why is it I feel so run down right now? Maybe I'm coming down with a bug.

'Well, I'm here, aren't I?' I retort sarcastically. Then I look down at the floor, suddenly feeling ashamed. I'm not embarrassed that he's caught me. I'm more just upset with myself that I let this happen. That my sex drive took over the sensible side of my brain yet again.

He steps closer, his navy Vans in my vision. His forefinger pushes my chin up so I'm forced to look at him. The power of his eyes hypnotises me again, pulling me under his spell. How is this happening? Maybe he's a wizard or something and has actually put a spell on me.

He smiles sadly. 'You're worth so much more.'

My heart beats rapidly in my chest. What is it with him and his need to tell me I deserve better? And does he mean him? By the way he's staring into my soul right now, I'd guess yes, but I don't know him enough to just assume that.

Instead I pull away and escape as fast as my legs will take me.

Nicholas

I don't understand why she interests me so much, but she does. There's something intriguing about her. She acts fierce to everyone but there's a vulnerability deep down in her eyes. She only ever lets it show for mere seconds, before covering it back up, but it's there.

Something to tell me there's more to the brash, *sleep with as many men as possible* persona she puts out. I mean, aren't girls supposed to like all that chocolate and flowers shit? Not this bird.

It's almost as if she's self-destructive. She knows Tom's a dick, yet she still carries on sleeping with him. I mean, the guy came all the way from Peterborough to see her and ended up shagging some random redhead in the toilets. He's always had a thing for redheads. For most girls that would be game over, but not for Brooke.

When Tom was bragging, telling me yesterday that he was gonna booty call Brooke, I laughed. I thought she'd laugh in his face and tell him to fuck off. So, when she arrived I was floored. Is she that self-destructive?

She had the grace to look ashamed this morning and so she should be. She's worth so much more and deserves better than him. Brooke needs someone to look after her. Someone who builds her up, not uses and abuses her. *She needs me.*

Wait, fuck. Where did that come from? Do I want that person to be me? Fuck knows. All I know is that I feel ridiculously protective of her for some reason. Maybe it's the sadness I see behind her eyes. It mirrors my own.

Chapter 4

Tuesday 1st August

I'm one of those irritating people that starts getting excited for their birthdays six months before the event. I know it must be annoying, but hey, you're only born once, right?! Today, I'm turning the grand old age of twenty-seven. And I feel old. I know Erica and Evelyn are way older, but I still feel so close to thirty. Not that I don't still look hot. I do. But that doesn't mean it's not freaked me out slightly.

I get woken up at 10am by all the girls bringing me croissants and jam, with coffee bought from Costa. It's amazing. They surround me on the bed handing over their cards and presents. It's unbelievable I'm lucky enough to call them family.

For so many years I dreaded my birthday because it just meant another day of being widely ignored by my mum and sisters. Sometimes Mum would give me a card with a fiver in it, but I never felt like she was happy to celebrate another year of my life.

Not these girls. These girls have taken a day off work just so they can shower me in their love. How did I get so lucky?

'So, what's my surprise today?' I ask, barely able to conceal my excitement.

They never let me plan anything myself. It's something we do for all of us actually and I know from when we've organised stuff for the others that a lot of thought goes into it. I still remember how long it took us to organise Erica's retro Sylvanian Family party.

'Well,' Erica divulges, bouncing on her bum. 'We know you're a big Walking Dead fan.'

'Who isn't?' I laugh. God, just the idea of Rick and Daryl in a Brooke sandwich has me salivating.

'So,' Alice beams, 'we're doing a zombie survival experience.'

My mouth drops open. 'No way!' I look to the others for clarification. They all nod, huge smiles on their faces. 'No way! That's fucking amazing!'

'It is my little sugarplum,' Molly says, jumping behind me to French plait my hair. 'Which is why you need to get your arse in gear.'

'Yep,' Evelyn nods, looking at her watch. 'We need to be leaving for London within the hour.'

'London's calling!' I sing, my mouth already aching from how huge I'm grinning. I fucking love going to London. 'Damn, did I ever tell you I love you girls?'

I'm interrupted by my phone flashing up with my Nan's care home number. It's either her wanting to wish me a happy birthday or they're calling to tell me she's ill. Or worse, done something weird. Again. That woman just can't stay out of trouble.

'Hello?' I answer apprehensively.

'Brooke, sweetheart,' Nan says fondly down the phone. 'Happy birthday to you!' She starts singing the whole happy birthday song while I let the others know it's Nan.

'Thanks, Nan. How are you feeling?'

'Much better now. It'll take some trying to get rid of me,' she chuckles. 'Well, I don't want to distract you from your birthday fun. I just wanted you to know how much I love you.'

Ah, she can be so cute sometimes. How she birthed my monster of a mother I'll never know.

'That and,' she lowers her voice to a whisper, 'to tell you that Sheila down the hall had sex with Billy downstairs.'

'What?' I gasp. I thought these old people were being watched?

'Yep. I'm quite jealous to be honest with you. I'm

far better looking than Sheila and I didn't even get a look in.'

Oh my God.

'Nan, are people even allowed to have sex there?'

She scoffs. 'It's not a prison, Brooke. We're allowed to live our lives.'

'O... kay.' Wait, does that mean *she* wants to have sex with Billy? 'You don't fancy this Billy though, right?'

'Don't be ridiculous,' she tuts.

Oh, thank the Lord.

'If I'd be getting jiggy with anyone around here, it'd be Geoff.'

Jesus Christ! Way to ruin my birthday.

We arrive at the abandoned looking compound already dressed in our sports gear and trainers. Better to be prepared. We knock on the door, not sure if we've got the right place.

'This is the address they gave us,' Evelyn says with a frown, consulting her printout.

The door suddenly opens abruptly, a huge guy with a buzz-cut dressed in army gear standing in front of us.

'Come in. Quickly!' he shouts, making us all jump. He shoos us in. 'Did you pass any of the infected on your way here?'

Wow, so he's going straight into character immediately. This is so cool!

'No,' Molly giggles, jumping excitedly from foot to foot. 'We're fine.'

'But if you want to check us for bites you can,' I add, fluttering my eyelashes seductively and leaning over to expose my cleavage. He's bloody gorgeous.

'No need, Ma'am. You'll be checked in the next room.'

God, he's really not breaking character. We go where directed into another room where our bags are taken off us. We actually *are* searched for bite marks and then we're lined up and sprayed with freezing cold water straight out of a hose.

'Fuck!' I screech, my nipples immediately like ice. 'Thanks for my present, girls.'

Evelyn's screaming so much she definitely didn't hear me. The guy seems to be blasting her more than us as if pleased by her agony. It makes me laugh. There's no way any of us saw this coming.

'Right,' the guy shouts at us, 'now that you've been decontaminated you can move into the next area.'

'Hopefully, we'll be able to grab a coffee in there,' Erica says with a grin, squeezing the water out of her hair.

No such luck. In there we're thrown together with another group of people, some all the way up to their fifties. Shit. I hope they don't have heart attacks. I suppose that's why we had to sign that disclaimer.

'Right,' another army guy at the front shouts. 'You are the survivors of the South East. It is up to *us* to take it back. Right now, we're going to train you in shotgun use. In the next room, we have some zombies we can practise on. Only the strong will survive. Shoot for the head and don't hesitate.'

God, it's bloody thrilling! It all feels so real.

Learning how to use the guns is amazing even though I'm not even a gun person. I can imagine Rick or Daryl being proud of how I handle it. There'd be boners all round.

'This is it,' army guy shouts next to the slide metal door before he opens it. 'Ready?'

I look to the others. Evelyn and Alice look determined while Molly and Erica look terrified. It makes me chuckle.

The doors are opened and we're thrown into an abandoned warehouse full of blood thirsty zombies wearing such good make-up I'd swear it was real if I didn't know. They start coming at us quickly, clawing at our clothes. We start shooting like mad, the shots assaulting my ears as one by one of they go down.

Erica gets cornered by one. Just as I'm about to save her she goes fucking nuts, slapping and punching at the zombie like a woman possessed. Crap. I run over and grab her from behind, trapping her hands down by her sides.

'It's not real, Erica,' I shout over the noise.

The lights suddenly come up. All the zombies are now down. I look around, adrenaline coursing so hard I can barely hear. Lots of people that came in with us are lying on the floor. What's happened?

I glance back at the other girls. They're all standing. All except Molly. She's huddled in a corner rocking back and forth with her eyes closed. Bless her.

'I think you broke my nose, you crazy bitch!' Erica's "zombie" shouts, clutching at it.

'Danielle!' the army guy shouts. 'I told you not to break character!' Danielle storms off. 'Congratulations, girls. It seems you're the only survivors. Please come with me for a second briefing.'

'Woo, we rock!' Alice shouts, high-fiving me. Someone's clearly pumped from the adrenaline.

We're brought into another room. How many bloody rooms does this place have?

'Now, we're going to meet up with the Cambridgeshire sector survivors. Together we'll plan our attack.'

The door opens and in walks Jack, Tom, Nicholas and Charlie. What the hell are they doing here?

Jack gives Erica a quick kiss.

'How did you guys know we were here?' I ask no one in particular.

Charlie smiles. 'Erica's had this booked for weeks. To be fair, we had to survive the first half and apparently you guys were betting against us surviving it.'

Alice grins. 'You can't blame us. I remember how you reacted to a jellyfish on Luna Island.'

Charlie sticks his tongue out.

'We have no time for this!' the army guy shouts. 'We need to make a plan.'

Nicholas steals a glance over at me. What is it about his looks? He has such bloody intense eyes. I feel like every time he glances at me it's as if he's burning something into my skin.

The army guy gets out a map and starts going on about how we plan to leave the compound, pick up emergency supplies and make it to the helicopter. I can't help but be mad at the girls for involving the guys. I thought this was girls only day. Not something to be ruined by testosterone. I was looking forward to spending time alone with Erica, but that's out of the window now that Jack's here.

Before I have time to give myself a pep talk and warn Erica not to beat the ever-living shit out of anymore actors, the doors to outside are flung open. The cool air hits my face, reminding me I have to get out of my head and spring into action.

We run towards the area that has the supplies, but as expected zombies are all over the place. Molly screams hysterically as they surround us. Yeah, she's not going to last long.

I start shooting while attempting to make my way to the supplies tent. It's a lot harder to shoot people in the head than you'd think, especially when they're moving towards you with their terrifying make up.

I finally get to the tent just as I run out of bullets. I look around for refills, but all I can find are sacks labelled food, water and weapons. In the weapons sack it's just a few knives. Shit. I look back at the others to see that Molly, Alice, Evelyn and Charlie are already down.

Suddenly, I'm thrown to the floor. I turn to see a zombie leaning over clawing at me, attempting to bite. Shit, it all looks so real, I can't help but completely freeze up. I use my hands to hold it off me, but this bitch is strong and so in character, her teeth snapping together. She should get some kind of zombie Oscar or something.

I scramble behind me for some kind of weapon, a stick or something. Why didn't I grab a knife while I could? A knife suddenly goes through the zombie's head. Well, one of the pretend knives they supply that go in when they make contact with something. It looks scarily real. I realise that it's Tom who saved me. My hero.

Not for long. A zombie fake bites him in the neck. They have crept up behind him, attaching his orange sticker to show he's now out of the game.

'Shit, sorry,' I apologise as I run away from him with the bag of weapons and food.

I look to see the guys already loading onto the helicopter. I cannot believe they're using a real helicopter. Shit, how much did the girls shell out for this? I use a knife in the sack to stab a few zombies, but the time it takes me means that the helicopter is starting to take off with Nicholas, Jack and Erica in it. Shit, I'm too late.

I run to it and attempt to jump on, but it's too high. Shit, the zombies are going to get me. They seem to be shouting at the pilot to slow down but it's not stopping. Nicholas suddenly jumps down. What the hell is he doing? He grabs me round the waist and hikes me up towards it. Jack and Erica grab me to help me on. I turn around just in time to see Nicholas taken down by a zombie.

'Nooooo!' I scream.

'Babe,' Erica says, touching my arm. 'You do realise this is fake right?'

My breathing is laboured, my eyes wide in horror. 'Oh yeah,' I shrug. 'Of course.'

Once the helicopter has landed and we've washed off the dirt and kill marks, we're led back outside and given some orange squash and a biscuit as if we've just given blood. It is crazy how utterly exhausted I feel now that all the adrenaline has worn off.

I can't get over how Nicholas sacrificed himself to save me. Yes, I know it was all make believe, but in the moment, it felt so real. I can't help but wonder if it felt real to him. He's over by the biscuits, hovering awkwardly, as if he's genuinely having a hard time deciding between custard creams or hobnobs. I have to say something to him.

Smiling at Molly, who seems to still be recovering from the whole experience with Alice, I walk over towards him. I can tell he notices me approaching. His body language changes as if he's on high alert.

I take an extra hobnob and attempt an awkward smile.

'So, thanks for saving my life back there,' I offer with a pathetic laugh after it. God, I hate myself sometimes.

He smiles briefly before covering it up with his normal indifferent stare. 'You're welcome. Except, if this was a real situation I'd have already taken my emergency supply of bullets and be halfway to Mexico.'

I burst out laughing. 'Oh yeah, reckon you'd be organised, do you?' I tease.

'Please,' he scoffs. 'I'm always listening out on the news for stories they're covering up and making out to be no big deal. If anyone's prepared I am. Daryl's got nothing on me.'

'Wait, you watch the Walking Dead?'

He scoffs as if I've just said something ridiculous. 'Of course, I watch it. People that don't are fucking morons.'

'Right!' I agree with a laugh. This is actually the most ever I've talked with him.

'Brooke!' Erica shouts over. 'We need to leave now if we're going to make our afternoon tea reservation.'

We're having afternoon tea? That's amazing! I love those stupid tiny sandwiches and I'm so glad to hear we're going back to some girlie time.

'Have fun,' he says, a hint of a smile on his lips.

I wink back at him. 'I always do.'

God, I'm absolutely shattered. So shattered I nearly fell asleep in the bath after washing what seemed like never-ending fake blood off my arms. We got some funny looks at afternoon tea. But I forced myself to get dressed and turn up.

My regular shag, Joshua, has insisted on taking me out tonight. I considered trying to get out of it, but I suppose a free dinner and being spoilt isn't all that bad. I really fancy chocolate covered strawberries tonight and I have more chance of getting them here than in my bedroom.

It turns out he's booked us into quite a fancy restaurant. We bypass the normal tables and are led by the suited waiter towards the back of the room and up a winding staircase. We're seated at a table in the middle of the room. No one else is around, all other tables only made up with their black tablecloths and tea-light candles. Well, this is weird.

'Are we the only booking up here?' I ask the waiter.

He glances quickly to Joshua. 'Yes, Madam.'

Did I just imagine it or did they exchange something with their eyes?

'Okay,' Joshua says glancing to me with an affectionate smile. 'Shall we start with a bottle of Prosecco?'

'Sounds good to me.'

I wait for him to order himself a beer, but he instead looks at his menu. I've never trusted straight guys that drink Prosecco. Like guys that wear leather driving gloves. It's just weird.

'So,' he says, gazing at me adoringly. It worries me

when he does that. 'How has your day been?'

'Amazing,' I beam, a host of memories invading my mind. The strongest one involving Nicholas' arms around my waist as he basically threw me on that helicopter. 'We had a zombie experience in London. Was so much fun. But now I've sat down I realise how knackered I am.'

I'm hoping he'll offer to get the meal to go. That way we can eat the food at his place and follow it with lazy sex.

He seems shocked. 'I never knew you liked zombies.'

'There's a lot you don't know about me,' I say with a wink.

The truth is that he's constantly trying to find out more about me. Always asking annoying questions, trying to turn himself into my boyfriend. I tell him as politely as I can that it's better the less we know about each other and move on. Even if I was looking for a boyfriend, it definitely wouldn't be Joshua. He's far too clingy. I only keep him around because he's amazing in the sack.

The waiter delivers our Prosecco. I deliberately take a huge gulp. I have a feeling I'm gonna need it to get through this evening.

'So...' he grins excitedly. 'How long have we been seeing each other now?'

I roll my eyes. Why is he always trying to get us to be serious? 'Well, we've been *shagging* now for about... God, I don't know. Maybe six months?'

'Eight months,' he smiles lovingly, taking my hand in his.

God, I need to cut this guy loose. He definitely wants more and I am not feeling it.

'Has it really been that long?' I ask, taking another few glugs of my drink.

'Yep,' he nods, 'and I've come to see you as an integral part of my life.'

Oh Jesus. This is awkward. I really don't have the energy right now to have this conversation again.

'You're the first thing I think of in the morning and the last thing at night.'

Oh God. This is awful. Why did I ever think I could keep it just sex with him? *Because he is amazing at going down on me.* Yeah, there is that.

'Yeah... listen,' I start, fighting back the tiredness and Prosecco haze to break it to him gently. I wish he'd have said this after our meal. I've heard the steak is amazing, and I really wanted my chocolate covered strawberries.

'No.' He squeezes my hand. '*You* listen. You're the best thing that's ever happened to me, Brooke.'

I gulp. 'But...'

He covers my mouth with one of his fingers. 'Sssh! Let me say this first.'

I hate being told to shut up but I nod begrudgingly through gritted teeth.

I take a large mouthful of Prosecco.

'I want you to be my wife, Brooke.'

My mouth drops open and basically touches the floor, dribbling out the Prosecco onto my dress.

I wipe my mouth. 'You... you what now?'

He drops to his knee. This cannot be happening! And on my birthday no less. At least there's no one else around to witness it.

'Marry me, Brooke, and make me the happiest man in the world.'

Oh my God. My whole life flashes before me. Married to this guy. 2.4 kids. Living in a house in the suburbs with a white picket fence and a dog with three legs and a limp.

'No.' There's no other way for me to answer.

Music suddenly blares out from speakers I had no idea existed. *Celebration* is playing. What the hell?

Balloons fall from the ceiling and a curtain beside us pulls away to reveal a crowd of people whooping and hollering, exploding party poppers in my face. What the hell is happening here? Is this a nightmare?

People are gushing in my face, saying their

congratulations. I look over at Joshua. He looks crestfallen. The people are also slapping him on the back. Wait, are they... his family? That's when it hits me. He's had this planned the entire time.

The nutcase was so sure I'd say yes, he invited his family and friends to witness it. The excited bastards mustn't have heard my no. Well this is beyond awkward.

What do I do?

Fuck it, I don't have time to spare his feelings. I grab my bag, dodge the nutcases and run out of there like it's on fire. One thing's for sure. That's a regular screw gone down the toilet.

Chapter 5

Friday 4th August

By Friday I've heard nothing from either Tom or Nicholas, not that I was expecting to. Okay, maybe I was expecting a little text from Nicholas asking if I ached after the zombie thing.

I mean, am I imagining that he's into me? Maybe he's just being friendly. He's just so bloody confusing. Blowing hot one minute and cold the next. I need less of that in my life right now. Especially when I still haven't even got a bloody photo of my dad from Mum, let alone a name.

I've been calling her daily chasing for it, but she's always got some sort of excuse. It makes me wonder if she actually has a photo at all. I mean, maybe they were just a one-night bunk up and she's too ashamed to admit it. But something tells me that's wrong. The way she's always looked when I've talked about him. Brokenhearted. Despondent. Crushed.

Well, today this goes on no longer. I'm going around there and I'm going to root around her room until I find it.

With the gorgeous weather that's forecast, the boys are coming down again this weekend. I'm not sure how I feel about that. Because I'm not sure they realise it's Gay Pride.

I fucking love Pride. Everyone's out in rainbow colours, our very own resident lesbian, Molly, gets to march for her people and we all get smashed, watching the love surrounding us. But I have no idea how some lads from Peterborough are gonna handle that kind of madness.

I did actually consider trying to get out of it and booking myself a spa weekend somewhere. Just thinking about having to face Tom and Nicholas again has me squirming in awkwardness. Erica put a stop to any of those thoughts when she found me searching online and told me I'm not allowed to bail. And that bitch has the best puppy dog eyes around. Plus, we've always gone to support Molly.

But something tells me that if I just find a piece of the puzzle of my dad, I'll feel better about seeing them. About everything really. I can't help but admit that I've always felt a part of me is missing by not knowing anything about him.

I let myself into my old house calling for Mum. No response. They're probably out shopping or doing something ridiculous. That's all they seem to do: shop, sleep, spend their benefits or get trashed. Anyway, it's good news for me. Means I can root around uninterrupted.

I start in her bedroom, searching in all the usual places: her bedside cabinets, storage boxes on top of the wardrobe, even under the bed. But nothing, just a shit load of dust. The only other place I can think of to look is in the loft, but... spiders.

Oh God, Brooke. Man up and overcome it. If I get the answers I want, it'll have been worth the risk.

I use the stick to open the loft hatch and pull down the ladder. I tentatively climb up, taking a large deep breath before daring to flick the light on. The neglected loft comes to life. An array of old dusty boxes greets me. It's as chaotic as her life. Great.

I case the place for any sign of spider species. It seems clear enough. But then they always seem to hide, lurking in the corners until you least expect it. It's as if I can feel them crawling on my shoulders.

I grab a box, blowing off the dust and removing the lid to discover photo albums within. I thumb through them, but come up empty. Just a load of ugly baby photos of the terrible twosome.

The next box at first glimpse looks like old fancy dress outfits. I wonder if there's something I can wear for Pride?

Rummaging through I find notebooks at the bottom. I pick one up and rifle through it. It's filled with my mum's scrawled handwriting. I notice a date on one page and as I flick through I quickly realise it's a diary. My mum kept diaries? She SO does not seem like a diary keeping kind of woman.

I thumb through to the beginning to realise this was written about four years before I was born.

Before I know what I'm doing, I'm frantically opening the other books and checking the dates. This is *just* like Mamma Mia.

I finally find the dates I need: 1989 to 1990.

I make myself comfortable, well as comfortable as I can in this crap hole, trying to work out nine months before my birthday. One entry is titled *Met the Man of My Dreams!* Oh Mother. I'm embarrassed for her and brace myself for cringe city.

I've met him. The man of my dreams. I went for some drinks with the girls from work and there he was, standing at the bar in a suit and tie. He has black hair and piercing blue eyes. I was in love the minute I laid eyes on him.

I can't help but get a thrill at the idea that I look like him. Finally, I look like somebody. I don't know if I'm more shocked at that or the fact my mum once worked.

The girls dared me to go talk to him. And aren't I glad they did! He's just amazing. Such a sweet talker. He asked me out tomorrow night. I can't wait. His name is Jonathan and I'm pretty sure I'm in love.

I roll my eyes. God, she was an idiot. My leg starts cramping so I stand up and shake it around. I place it back down on the ground, but I fall, my foot going right through the ceiling. Fuck! What kind of shit arse ceiling does she have?

I try to pull it out again, but it seems to be wedged into the plaster. Fuck, it hurts, it's throbbing like mad. I'm probably going to have a million splinters from the floorboards.

Right, focus Brooke. I need to call someone. I look around for my phone. Damn, I'd put it by the box. I stretch out to get it using all the yoga I've ever done in my life, but I'm still a fraction too far away from it. Damn.

I look around for something to help me, but of course there's absolutely nothing. Bugger.

All I have is the diary in my hand. That'll have to do. I use it, stretching with all of my might, to hit the phone in my direction. It finally falls within reach, something falling out of the diary in the process. I don't have time for that now.

I speed dial Erica. It goes to answerphone. Are you fucking kidding me?! I try Alice but it just rings. She refuses to put an answerphone message on it because she doesn't want to pay for her messages. Molly should be about. She works at Brighton Zoo and carries her phone with her in case of a lion attack or something, so she should be able to answer an emergency call. It goes straight to answerphone. For fuck's sake girls!!

The only person left to try is Evelyn, and I really, *really* don't want to ask her of all people for help. I look down at my sunken leg. But beggars can't be choosers.

I take a deep breath and call her. She answers after the second ring. Of course she does, efficient cow.

'Hi, Brooke,' she answers, sounding a lot more chilled out than normal.

'Hi, Evie. I need your help.'

'Really?' Yes, yes, I think it's clear we're not usually that close. We're basically only friends through Erica, but I need her right now. 'What do you need?'

I sigh. How can I describe this without it sounding ridiculous? 'I've sort of got myself into a... situation. Can you drive to Castledean?'

'Castledean?' she repeats sceptically. 'What the hell are you doing there?'

Ugh, with the questions. 'I'm at my mum's house. And I've kind of got my leg stuck in the loft flooring.'

There's an eerie silence. What the hell is she thinking? An explosion of laughter nearly bursts my eardrums. I hold the phone away from me. 'Okay, give me the address.'

I reel it off. 'But you'll also have to break in as I obviously can't answer the door.'

'Where the hell is your mum?'

I sigh dramatically. 'Let's see. 2:30 pm on a Friday. She could be in a bar getting off with a stranger, in a shopping centre piling up more debt on her credit card or ruining people's dreams. The list is endless.'

There's an awkward pause. I've never divulged anything about my mum before. She's probably shocked.

'Okay, I'll be there as soon as I can.'

Good girl. I'm starting to see why Evelyn keeps her around. She might be a pain in the arse sometimes, but she's reliable as hell.

I try to reach for what fell out of the diary to pass the time. It looks like a Polaroid. I stretch but can't reach it. Oh well, back to the diary.

I went out with him tonight and ended up back at his. He is such a gentle lover.

Eww! I throw the book down like it's on fire. Too much information, Mother. Ugh.

I take a few calming deep breaths, only picking it back up when I feel brave enough. I skim through the next few pages as I really don't want to hear their bloody love story.

I stop when I see the word devastated underlined three times. Uh-oh. Heartbreak here we come.

I was so excited to tell him my news. We were going to be a perfect little family: him, me and peanut. Only when I told him over dinner last night he didn't drop to his knees, gush with excitement and ask me to marry him.

No, instead his face dropped and drained of all colour. He says we're too young for a baby. That we should consider getting rid of it. Getting rid of our baby! Is he nuts? If he loves me why wouldn't he want our baby? But then I suppose he hasn't actually told me he loves me yet, but I know he does. I see it in his eyes.

Jesus, young mum was a bit of a naïve nutter. Talk about a bunny boiler, but I understand that she must have been gutted. And I can't lie, it does sting to hear of my dad wanting to abort me so easily.

So now I have to decide what I want. Him or the baby. He says I can't have both. Devastated is an understatement.

Wow. So, he was an absolute arsehole. Imagine telling her to choose. I don't need to read anymore to see who she chose. I'm here, currently stuck with my leg in the ceiling.

It also makes sense why she always seemed to resent me so much. But I mean, over the years, surely she realised that what she had wasn't love? It was clear, even from her diary, that it was more infatuation. Your first love kind of thing.

Another example of why I need to stay away from relationships. They make you seriously dumb.

A little while later I hear the smashing of glass in the distance. Is that Evelyn breaking in? Please, God, I'm starting to lose the feeling in my leg.

'Evelyn?' I shout.

'We're coming,' she yells back.

We? Who the hell has she brought with her? Like this couldn't get any more embarrassing.

'Brooke?' I hear her shout up the loft stairs.

'Yes, who bloody else could it be?' I shout back in frustration.

Someone giggles. Oh God, it's Molly. I'd know those giggles anywhere. Molly's the first to climb up.

'Hey, hun, you look so funny!' She collapses over in hysterics while Evelyn climbs up. Helpful.

'Yeah, thanks for that,' I snap sarcastically. 'Don't worry about if I'm in any pain or anything.'

'Are you?' Evelyn asks, her brows furrowed in concern.

'Well, no, I'm okay,' I begrudgingly admit. 'Although my leg has gone completely dead now.'

Molly laughs. 'Okay. That means it's fine for a picture.' She stands in front of me, putting her phone in selfie mode. She pulls a funny face, pointing over her shoulder to me with my leg in the floor.

'That is *so* going on Insta,' she giggles. I growl at her, my jaw clenched in barely concealed rage. 'Don't worry, I'll tag you,' she smiles, as if she doesn't notice my mood. Just doesn't want to acknowledge it more like.

Evelyn starts to look around the leg. She nods to Molly, 'Just like I thought.'

Molly nods back, disappearing back down the stairs.

'Where's she going?'

'Brooke,' she says seriously. 'You have two options. One, we can call the fire brigade and they'll cut you out.'

'Sexy firemen? Yes please!' Finally, something good to come from this.

Her eyes widen. 'Okay, so you don't mind the embarrassment factor?'

Oh God, she's right. I'd never live it down. No doubt Molly would live stream the whole thing.

'What's the second option?'

'The second option is...' She looks towards Molly as she struggles to climb up with a sledgehammer. Why the hell does she have a sledgehammer? 'We do it ourselves.'

I shrink back. 'What the hell are you going to do with *that?'*

'Simple,' Evelyn explains, as if this is no big deal. As if friends get stuck in ceilings all the time. 'We're just going to bash out around it, loosen the plaster or whatever.'

I make a face. She doesn't sound convincing. 'And you reckon you can do this?'

'Easily,' Evelyn laughs, tapping the sledgehammer as if it's a pet dog.

Molly goes to swing it up behind her.

'Wait!' I scream, my hands above my head to protect me. 'How do I know you're not going to miss and break my leg?' I've seen this bitch playing rounders. She's not the best shot.

She cackles. 'You don't. You just have to trust me.'

'Fuck my life. Well, before you potentially traumatise me for life do me a favour and pass me that polaroid.' I point towards it.

She follows my pointing and gets it, having a quick look before handing it back to me. I slip it safely into my jeans pocket.

'Who's that guy? He looks like you.'

I shrug. 'Just an uncle. Anyway, are we doing this or not?'

'Let's do it.'

Evelyn stoops down onto her haunches, ready to wiggle my leg free, while Molly holds the sledgehammer behind her shoulder. Jesus, she looks terrifying.

She slams it down onto the floor, just managing to miss my leg. It vibrates, but nothing happens.

'It's gonna take another one,' she says, not missing a beat before slamming it down again. This time so hard that the floor cracks, my leg loosens, but so does the rest of the floor. We look at each other in wide eyed panic before we crash through the ceiling. Shit.

Something breaks my fall. I look around between the falling debris to see that I've landed on a double bed. Avery's bed to be exact. Well how the fuck did this happen?

'Shit,' Evelyn says, trying to clear her face of crap. 'What kind of crap arse ceiling do you have here?'

Molly starts laughing. 'This could seriously only happen to us.' She takes her phone out and takes a quick selfie of the three of us.

'Not the time for a picture, Molly,' Evelyn snaps.

The front door suddenly slams. 'Brooke!' Avery shouts up. 'I've told you I don't like you letting yourself in when we're not home!'

Oh fuck. Just when I thought it couldn't get any worse.

'Oh shit,' I gasp, looking around at them. 'She's going to kill me. Like *literally* kill me.'

Evelyn searches around the room frantically. 'Not if we get out first,' she says, a steely determination in her eyes.

I look down at my leg. It's cut slightly, throbbing and covered in crap. It looks like I'm not going to escape from this without an infection.

'I don't even know if I can walk,' I admit, trying to move it and wincing from the pain.

Molly stands in front of me pointing at my leg. 'On it.' She grabs me and throws me onto her shoulders, fireman style. How is she so bloody strong? She's so dainty.

Evelyn motions for her to follow her down the stairs. We creep slowly, trying to make as little noise as possible. From the banging of her boots I'd guess Avery's in the kitchen.

'Shit, Brooke!' she shouts up, making us all jump. 'Someone's broken in!'

'She must be looking at the window,' Evelyn whispers. Molly nods and immediately we're running for it, opening the front door and racing to my car. I unlock it before Molly throws us in the back, my leg stinging in pain.

Evelyn takes the wheel. She starts the engine and screeches out of there just as Avery comes running out with a face full of fury. We drive off with her attempting to chase us. Luckily that bitch has no cardio skills.

'Phew!' Molly cries, out of breath from the run. 'Now we just need to take you to hospital and you've been officially saved by James and Fielding! God, our surnames sound good together. We could totally have our own cop show.'

See, why would I need a man in my life when I have these crazy ride-or-die chicks at my side?

Chapter 6

Friday 4th August

The girls have just settled me on my bed when I hear Erica and Jack walk through the door.

'Ugh, how the hell am I gonna explain this?' I ask Evelyn and Molly, pointing towards my ripped jeans and swollen ankle.

'Are you sure we shouldn't get you to a hospital?' Evelyn asks with a frown. 'I have no idea how you plan on watching the parade tomorrow on that ankle.'

'I'm fine,' I snap. 'Besides, I haven't missed one since I've moved here and I'll be damned if I start now.'

Molly beams back at me. 'Plus, there's always a friendly gay willing to give a piggy back.'

I burst out laughing. She's right.

'Anyway,' Molly says, clapping her hands together. 'Let's go see the boys. Let them know what they're in for.'

I freeze. 'Sorry, what?'

'The guys...' she says looking at me as if I'm mad. 'They're due to arrive any minute.'

'Nuh-uh,' I argue like a child. 'They're coming tomorrow, right? Right?'

Erica walks into the room, all smiles. 'They're here!'

I stare at her in disbelief. 'The guys are here, *now?* I thought they were coming tomorrow.'

'No... tonight,' she nods as if she's already told me. 'And ssh, because we haven't told them it's Pride tomorrow.'

Evelyn rolls her eyes and shakes her head. 'How haven't they already figured it out with all the hotels booked up?'

Erica's eyes follow down to my leg. 'Shit, Brooke, what did you do to yourself?'

Molly chuckles. 'She decided to put her leg through her mum's loft floor.'

Erica narrows her eyes at me. 'What were you doing in the loft?'

Shit, she's the first one to ask why. The front doorbell rings and a second later guys voices fill the sitting room. Crap, they're here.

'No time for that now,' I insist, shooing her away. 'You best go tell them what they're in for.'

She nods, but looks at me with warning. I know the minute she gets me alone I'm in for a grilling. Her and the girls leave me to wallow in my own pitifulness.

I'm hoping to hide out here for as long as I can. The last time I saw Tom and Nicholas they were both attempting to be my hero at the zombie experience.

Ugh, this is why it's always so much easier to sleep with the little circle I keep. Those and the randoms I pick up along the way. They either know the score or I don't have to worry about seeing them again.

But then when I was shagging Tom on holiday I never thought we'd see any of them again. Let alone have them to stay in my own flat. Damn Erica for falling in love with Jack.

I really do need a shower though. I still have ceiling crap in my hair and I need to wash the cuts on my leg thoroughly. I take the polaroid out of my pocket and stare back at the man that never wanted me to enter this world.

A thump on the ground shakes me from my thoughts. I look up to see Nicholas has dumped his over-bulging duffle bag on the floor by my door, leaning against the doorframe with his arms crossed over his chest. He looks edible. God, why does he have to just linger though? I quickly stuff the picture into my bedside drawer.

'Alright?' I ask with a nod, forced to be the first one to talk.

He doesn't smile, just nods towards my leg. 'What happened?'

I sit up, feeling vulnerable being this close and alone with him in my bedroom.

'Oh nothing. Long story. Anyway, is everyone here?' I limp past him, so close I can smell his aftershave, but he takes my arm, halting me.

'You sure you're gonna be able to walk on that thing?'

I scoff, yanking his hand off me. 'That *thing* is my leg and yes, I'll be fine.' God, why does he always feel the need to fuss over me. It's beyond annoying.

I limp out to the others, just as Tom's being told where we're going tomorrow.

'Sorry, nuh-uh. I am *not* going to spend the day at Pride.'

I roll my eyes. He's such a Neanderthal.

'I didn't realise you were homophobic,' Evelyn says, arms crossed over her chest, 'as well as a manwhore.'

'Hey,' he insists, holding his hands up in surrender. 'I am not a homophobe. It's just that it's not safe for a pretty guy like me. I mean, it's like dangling some prime rib eye steak in front of some hungry hyenas and trying to tell them they can't have it.'

Erica bursts out laughing. 'So, what you're saying is that you're irresistible?'

We all join in laughing hysterically. After today I needed this laugh.

'And not only that,' Alice joins in, 'but every gay man is apparently gagging for it?'

'That's offensive to all my kind,' Molly joins in, winking with a snort so we know she's joking.

She's almost impossible to offend. Someone once called her a dyke and while I was ready to bottle the bitch, she just laughed and said she didn't really like that term. Then she joked that she preferred muff muncher. It was so funny, all the rage I felt just evaporated. We ended up drinking with them until 2am.

'All I'm saying,' he tries, 'is that I find it hard enough fighting the women off. Let alone adding in all the men.'

'Well man up, buttercup,' I say with a smile. 'Because that's where we're going.'

'In the meantime,' Molly sings, 'pizza party!'

Saturday 5th August

Last night was awkward to say the least. I hated having to walk back from the shower in just my towel. I could feel Tom watching me. Ugh, I am not going back there again.

Having all the guys crammed into our small flat was

ridiculous, but needs must. We knew it would be crazy trying to get a drink anywhere and all the restaurants were booked up so pizza party it was. Luckily, we booked a table months ago for tomorrow night at our favourite Italian restaurant and didn't have much of a problem adding four more to the table.

I steered clear of Nicholas and Tom for most of the night. Erica kept asking me why I was so quiet, but I blamed my leg, which I'd managed to clean up and bandage myself with our first aid kit. I knew I should have been a nurse.

I must have received over twenty missed calls from mum, obviously fuming over what I'd done to her ceiling. I had no idea how I would fix that.

So now, after a restless night's sleep, we're walking towards the main street donned in our rainbow colours and covered in body glitter. I have on a rose-gold sequinned boob tube exposing my *Love is Love* belly button charm, with a denim mini and heels.

I've drawn Pride flags on my cheeks and added glitter around my eyes so that they shine extra bright. This is just one of the reasons why I love Pride. Anything goes.

The parade is already in full swing by the time we arrive, the streets jam-packed. Men dressed as flowers, giant petals around their heads are walking singing along to the Spice Girls while the backdrop of a clear blue sky and calm turquoise sea add to the magical vibe.

On closer inspection, I notice they're actually vaginas. How bloody hilarious that I didn't spot it right away! Drag queens dressed up as medusas follow them, their wigs styled to look like snakes.

'Woo!' we shout, cheering them on.

Pride is amazing because no-one is considered strange or unusual. There is no normal. Nothing but good vibes, pumping out love and acceptance.

Everyone feels comfortable as themselves. There are no bitchy girls. No one is different. We're all equal in our search for love.

Placard's with *More Love, Less Hate* are thrust around us as people blow whistles so loud it's almost deafening. Brighton's Gay Men's Chorus' float has singing men dressed in seventies clothes, flower-head pieces and multi-coloured wigs. Bubbles shoot towards us.

I jump up over the crowds so I can see them and come down hard on my ankle.

Pain shoots up my leg from my ankle, blinding me temporarily.

'Fuck!' I hiss through my teeth.

When I can focus again I notice I'm on the floor. The girls are looking down at me with wide eyes while

Nicholas is already leaning down and scooping me up as if I weigh no more than a feather.

'Out of my way!' he's screaming, pushing against the hordes of people as if I'm on my deathbed.

'Nicholas, I'm fine,' I shout over the noise, my foot being bashed against someone's back. I flinch, scrunching my eyes shut.

'Yeah, looks like it,' he snorts.

He pushes through the crowds and through the parade of Adonis guys in nothing but a dickie bow and apron.

'Jesus, you can't just go *through* the parade!'

'Watch me,' he practically growls.

I roll my eyes. This guy cannot be told what to do. Stubborn bloody mule.

'Where are you taking me, anyway? The flat's back that way.' I point behind him noticing a red double decker bus with an inflatable peace symbol at the front as it drives past decorated with Pride-coloured balloons. The top is off and people are dancing, waving their flags in celebration. Why did I have to hurt my stupid ankle?

'I'm not taking you back to the flat.'

I try to struggle out of his hold but there's no way he's letting me anywhere so I decide to just go with it. Anyway, I'm in too much pain right now to try to argue over the noise of woos and whistles.

'Here!' he suddenly shouts to someone. 'She's hurt her ankle.'

I look over his shoulder to see he's brought me to the paramedic's tent. God, he's resourceful.

He places me down onto a chair where a hairy faced paramedic that's dyed his beard the Pride rainbow colours takes hold of my foot.

'Okay, what happened here then?' hairy paramedic asks, taking my ankle gently in his hand.

I go to explain, but instead notice a man in the crowd watching me. He stands out because he's looking at me rather than facing the parade. Plus, he's not wearing any Pride colours, just jeans and a grey t-shirt.

I frown, squinting to see him closer, but just like that he's gone. Well that was bloody weird.

'Hello?' Hairy paramedic says, clicking his fingers in front of my face.

I turn to him. 'Sorry,' I shake my head. 'I thought I saw someone.'

He looks to Nicholas. 'She may be going into shock.'

'I'm not going into bloody shock!'

Hairy paramedic rolls his eyes but lets me tell him how it happened. He's basically useless, telling me he thinks it's just a sprain and to keep it moving. Here I was thinking you got crutches for sprains. Nope, this nutcase wants me to go run a marathon.

'Thank you,' I tell him begrudgingly as he helps me limp back over to our friends.

A pink float with sequinned WE LOVE BRIGHTON at the top drives past, full of the best-looking drag queens in town. Next up is an old man with a grey beard long enough to pass as Father Christmas on his mobility scooter. He has a sign attached to him that reads *I'm the oldest gay in the village.* Nicholas spots it and raises his eyebrows at me as if to ask *really?* We both burst out laughing.

'Why are you so arsey about me helping you, anyway?' he asks with a smile that slowly builds.

I huff, trying and failing to calm myself down. 'Sorry. I just hate asking for help.'

He pauses to study me with overly curious eyes. 'You mean you hate appearing vulnerable?'

'I'm not vulnerable!' I almost shout. His eyebrows bunch together, making me feel like a right drama queen. I sigh, trying to release some of the tension I always seem to feel around him. 'Okay, maybe you're right. I just hate relying on other people.'

He looks at me, poking his tongue into his cheek. 'How have you ever had any kind of relationship with that attitude?'

I snort. 'I haven't.' He tilts his head to the side and purses his lips. 'I mean, obviously I have my girls. But I don't do boyfriends. I get what I need and move on.'

He raises one eyebrow, giving me a glassy stare. 'Sounds lonely.'

'It's really not. I get what I want and don't have to put up with a guy's bullshit.'

'If you insist.'

We make it back to the others, Erica grabbing me as soon as she sees us. She drags me over to GAP where there's a woman in sequinned hot pants waving a rainbow scarf around to the music pumping in their window display.

'Brooke, what the fuck is going on? Why were you even at your mum's?'

She knows I wouldn't be there unless I needed to be. Erica knows everything about my relationship with her. If you can even call it a relationship.

I pretend to be distracted by the dancing woman, avoiding eye contact with her. 'I was just looking for something.'

Her face tightens. 'For what?'

My pulse quickens. I still haven't told her about looking for my dad and right now is definitely not the time.

'God, Erica, can't I have any secrets from you?'

She balks, clearly hurt. 'Sorry. I just... I was worried.'

Well now I feel like shit. 'I know. I'm sorry. Let's just ignore that and enjoy the weekend, okay?'

She nods, still not happy. 'Okay, but we *will* be talking about this again.'

Later that night, after enjoying a concert with Louisa Johnson in Preston Park and drinking far too much vodka at the Pride Village Party on James street, we're in the romantic Italian restaurant we booked.

Having drunk a bottle of wine on top of all that vodka I can't help but feel horny. Tom keeps touching my leg under the table, but I move it away before it progresses. I hope he's getting the hint.

He's really annoying me tonight. He's obviously wanting more sex, but I'm so over him. It's not him I want, it's Nicholas. I can't believe it's taken me so unbelievably long to realise it, but he's the one for me. I want every strange, twisted, tattooed piece of him.

Then I see him walk towards the toilets. Now's my chance. Away from everyone. I need to speak to him.

I limp into the corridor and lean against a wall, pulling my phone out so as not to look like a mental stalker lady. Which apparently, I've turned into. I'm definitely my mother's daughter. God, I shudder at the thought.

He walks out of the men's toilets and spots me, his lip quirking up for a second. I've known him enough to know that's his version of a smug smile.

'Hi,' I say awkwardly.

'Hi.' He folds his arms across his chest and leans against the opposite wall. 'So how come you're rebuffing Tom tonight?'

God, can he really be that dumb? Isn't it obvious how into him I am?

I bite my lip playfully. 'Maybe I don't like him anymore.'

'Oh yeah.' His eyebrows raise, his lips parting. 'Why's that?'

I twirl my hair, knowing it naturally draws attention towards my boobs. His eyes travel down. Bingo.

'Maybe I like someone else,' I offer playfully.

He freezes, staring at me aghast. Well, I didn't expect this reaction. His eyes become pained.

'You don't want someone like me,' he warns, his voice gravelly.

'Why not?' I can't help but blurt out.

Apparently, I have no pride left.

He scratches his right hand. 'Because I'm no good for you. You deserve...'

'Yeah, yeah,' I interrupt, 'I deserve *more*. Or so you

keep telling me. So why can't I have you?'

He looks at the floor, rubbing the back of his neck. 'It's for the best.'

What the fuck is his problem? Always trying to rile me up only to shoot me down.

'Yeah, well you know what? Fuck you, Nicholas.' I spin on my heel and storm back to the table.

Nicholas

Well I fucked that up, didn't I? I didn't want this to happen. I didn't want her to start liking me. Because I'm not good for her. Not with my history. She needs a normal relationship. A normal guy to take care of her. Not someone obsessive and controlling like me. Yet I can't stay away from her. She's addictive. She clearly has a huge heart. Team that with a dirty mind and its basically my ideal woman.

I'd suffocate her for sure and I know that as soon as I'd allow myself to feel her, really feel her, there'd be no going back for me. And she couldn't handle it.

Better that she stays away from me. Even if it pisses her off.

But this isn't how I wanted it to go down. I didn't want her to feel rejection. Something tells me she's had enough rejection in her life and the last thing I want is for me to add to it. For me to push her into the arms of another ungrateful man.

God, the thought of her being with someone else makes me clench my fist in rage. But I have to remind myself this is my fault. I'm the one who told her to stay away. I just hope I can take my own advice.

Brooke

Once we've finished up with dinner, we're back out and joining the swarms of people crowded onto the beach. It's now dark, the illuminated pier looking beautiful in the distance. Even though it's dark, the sky still seems to be blue, just now a darker version, a few clouds framing the moon. The fireworks start, everyone oohing and aahing as they reach up so high it's as if they touch it.

A girl walks past in just her knickers, a camisole and her boobs decorated in nothing but glitter. Her nipples are barely covered. Damn it, I knew I should have done that. She looks awesome. The guy's eyes nearly pop out of their head.

I look over to Jack and Erica. He doesn't even seem to have noticed glitter tits. He's got his arms wrapped around Erica from behind, in their own little world. She looks so content, the pure picture of happiness. I look over to Nicholas to find him already staring at me. It makes me shiver, wishing I could have his arms around mine.

'Cold there, babe?' Tom shouts in my ear.

He makes me jump. Before I have a chance to respond with anything he's copying Jack and wrapping his arms around me. Oh shit. Well, this doesn't look good in front of Nicholas. Not that I should care, I remind myself. He doesn't want me.

I chance a look at him. His legs are planted wide, his chin high. He cracks his knuckles, avoiding my stare. He's pissed for sure. Well, I might as well give him something to be pissed about.

I allow myself to relax into Tom's warm arms. He pulls me in tighter, resting his chin on my shoulder. It's not completely terrible.

'You're still not getting any,' I shout over my shoulder.

He laughs. 'Don't ruin the moment, babe.'

Chapter 7

Sunday 6th August

I still can't believe that dickwad Nicholas. Winding me up by flirting outrageously, building up my self-esteem only to shoot me down. Is he some sort of sadistic bastard or something? And turning down this premium steak. Like, *hello!* Well, I'm over it. I do not have time for any unnecessary drama in my life. No, thank you.

My phone buzzes with a text. It's Nicholas. Ugh, I can't help but be excited. What the hell is wrong with me?

You got the wrong end of the stick last night. It's not that I don't want you. It's that I'm not good for you.

Oh God, bore off! I hate when guys try to use that excuse. That whole "it's not you it's me" kind of thing. What a pussy. If you don't want me just be straight with me. Or better yet, just leave me the hell alone!

I wander into the kitchen to find Erica and Jack bickering about who put jam residue back into the butter. I swear, they're the only two adults I know that still make jam sandwiches. They were made for each other.

'It definitely wasn't me!' she protests, hand on her hip. 'I *always* do butter first, then jam.'

'Well so do I,' he counters, staring right back at her.

She glares back at him, practically growling.

He grins, breaking the tense body language. 'God, you look cute when you put on that mad little face.'

She tries hard to remain stern but within seconds she's crumpling into a laugh. 'You're *such* a dick,' she laughs, walking into his outstretched arms for a kiss.

I roll my eyes. 'Jesus, you two need to get a room,' I can't help but snap as I make my way to the fridge. 'Oh wait, you already have one.' I smile to let them know I'm joking. Half joking. I do wish they'd keep the PDA to a minimum.

'Where have you been all morning?' she asks, forehead creased. 'The boys wanted to say goodbye, but you'd locked your door.'

Duh. Of course, I did. I was clearly hiding.

'Had I?' I say vaguely, staring into the fridge so I don't have to look at her. I didn't want to see anyone this morning. Especially with how hungover I'm feeling.

'Yeah.' She narrows her eyes. 'Who upset you last

night? After you went to the loo, you came back to the table in a total mood.'

'I just felt sick.' She really needs to get off my back. I'm not feeling like an interrogation right now.

'Okay,' she says with an eye roll. 'I'm getting in the shower.' She kisses Jack on the cheek and walks away. He watches her go, checking out her arse.

I put some pop tarts in the toaster, trying to ignore the burning questions dancing around my mind. I can't help but get the desire to ask him about Nicholas. The urge is strong.

'So, what's the deal with Nicholas?' I ask nonchalantly, grabbing a plate out of the cupboard.

He looks up from the paper with a frowned forehead. 'What do you mean, his deal?'

I shrug, as if I haven't been dissecting everything about him since we've met. 'I mean why is he always so moody, sloping around like a teenager.'

He shrugs, not meeting my eyes. 'That's just what he's like.'

I bloody hate that excuse. No one is ever born that way.

'Yeah, but *why?* I mean did something happen to make him that way?'

Jack quickly looks away, readjusting his backside on his seat, his naked shoulders taut. Why the sudden tension? 'Look, I just know he's a good guy.'

'I'm right, aren't I? Something happened to him to make him like that?' It's the only explanation.

He puts his palms up in surrender. 'Look, it's not my story to tell, okay? If you want to know something ask him yourself.' He gets up and makes his way to the bathroom, no doubt to sneak peen attack Erica.

Damn it, why did he have to make him more bloody mysterious to me?

I made my way to Nan's home in a bid to distract myself. Not just from Nicholas, but from whether or not I should call a private detective to find my dad. I reckon she'll cheer me up. She always does.

She's not in her room so I go looking for her, finally finding her in the communal room sharing a private joke with some old dude.

'Nan,' I call to announce myself.

Every old lady in the place turns around to look at me. Ah, I suppose they're all nans at this age.

'Brooke,' she says in surprise, opening her arms wide. She engulfs me into a warm hug, her crepey skin pressing against my cheek. She always smells like talcum powder.

I look over at the guy who seems to be peering at me

with interest.

'Oh, how rude of me,' she blusters, giggling like a girl. 'Brooke, this is my friend Geoff.'

Shit. This is Geoff. The Geoff she basically admits to fancying.

This is weird.

'Hi,' I grumble curtly, not offering my hand. I size him up. Look at him with his purple cardigan. He's clearly a player in this place.

Nan looks at me with furrowed brows. 'Please excuse us, Geoff.' She takes my arm and starts leading me away. 'There's no need to be rude to the poor man,' she whisper-hisses at me.

'Sorry, Nan, but it creeps me out. You're too old to be chasing dick like that.'

'Brooke!' she laughs, as we make it inside her room. 'You know I'd never really do anything. I'll always love your grandfather.'

I smile. It does make me feel better knowing she wouldn't get with anyone else. Maybe I am an old romantic at heart. Somewhere deep, *deep* inside.

'Anyway, I want to hear all about Pride.'

I fill her in on the events, obviously leaving out the parts with Nicholas and Tom. Oh, and breaking through mum's attic floor. Nan apparently petitioned for the home to celebrate Pride. It's still decorated with rainbow bunting. She made them have a disco and danced with Sheila to YMCA. It sounded like a riot. Well, for this place anyway.

'I do worry that you hang around with too many gays,' she mutters, thoughtfully looking out of the window.

I know her well enough to know she doesn't mean any offence. She's just worried I'm never going to get married if I keep hanging around with men who are into other men.

'Trust me, Nan. I hang around with *plenty* of single men too.'

She waggles her eyebrows. 'But are you getting any?'

I burst out laughing. 'Nan!'

'What?' she laughs.

'Most nans are pressuring their grandaughter's for an engagement. You want to know if I'm having sex.'

'Well... are you?'

I blush. 'Jeez, yes, okay?'

'Good,' she nods, pleased with my answer. 'I just want you to live your life to the fullest, Brooke. I'm not even sure if marriage is for you. You were born to dance to the beat of your own heart. You're a free spirit, my little wild child and I want you to stay wild and free for as long as you can. Trust me, you're a long time married.'

Talk about sending me mixed signals.

'You're so confusing, Nan! It wasn't long ago you were telling me I need a man in my life.'

'I never said you had to marry him.' She winks and cackles a dirty laugh.

God, I love her.

Monday 7th August

I've called in and told work I have a dodgy stomach and that I'll be late in. No-one ever likes to question diarrhoea. The truth is I have an appointment with a private detective. I found one online that gives a free consultation. I feel like I need to talk it out. Even though I'm scared of what I'm going to find.

I walk into the old building and tell the receptionist I have an appointment. I wait on the squeaky faux leather sofa tapping my fingers restlessly. Do I really want to meet this man? The man that wanted me aborted? I still don't know. But I'm here now.

'Miss Archer?' the receptionist calls. 'He's ready for you now.'

I smile and follow her to a nearby door. I'm surprised the whole place seems this classy. I was kind of expecting a back-street place with an overweight, sweaty, balding guy. Not that I've met him yet.

The assistant opens the door and I'm greeted by a well dressed gentleman in his early fifties. Well, this is all going better than I thought.

'Miss Archer,' he smiles, shaking my hand firmly. 'Please take a seat and tell me a bit about your case.'

I take a deep breath, fiddling with the photo in my purse. 'I want to find my dad. All I have is this photo and that his name is Jonathan.' I hand it over.

He takes it and scribbles on his notepad. 'Okay, so no surname. Do you have an approximate age and location?'

'I know that he was in Brighton sometime in the late eighties/early nineties.'

'Okay,' he nods. 'Without more information, it can be hard to give you a proper quote for how much this will cost as we're unsure of the time restraint. But we can start work on a £200 retainer and if I see myself going over that I will contact you and ask how you'd like to proceed.'

'Wow. Okay, that sounds good.'

I was expecting for him to try to rip me off.

'Great. I'll get started on it right away and call you as soon as I have any news.'

Well that was all a lot more straightforward than I thought it would be!

I shake his hand again and walk out to the car park. My phone rings in my pocket. It's Mum. Crap. I suppose I have to face her sooner or later.

'Hi, Mum,' I say unenthusiastically.

'Brooke! What the hell have you done to my ceiling?' she shrieks.

Well, there's no good way to say this is there? 'I'm sorry. I was in the loft and I fell through. It was a total accident.'

'Well, now you're going to have to fix it! I can't afford to have it done. I called the council, but they threatened to evict me if I've deliberately done damage to the property. Brooke, I need you to sort this shit out.'

I roll my eyes even though she can't see me.

'Where on earth do you think I'm going to get that sort of money?'

'I don't know, Brooke. You're the one with the fancy degree and snazzy job. You should have a solution for this.'

'Ugh, fine. Look, get a few quotes from builders to fix it and then let me know the price.'

'Fine,' she snaps. 'But I still don't hear a sorry, Brooke.'

I feel my blood turn into fire.

'Sorry I had to go into your loft so I could find some kind of information on my own father which you refuse to give me.'

There's silence on the other end. 'I've told you before, Brooke. He's better left in the past.'

'Why? Because he wanted to abort me?'

I hear the sharp intake of breath. 'How do you know that?'

'I found your diary, Mum.'

'You read my diary?' she shrieks, like a teenage girl.

'Yes, I read your diary.' I steel myself for a moment, reminding myself that she chose my life over the love of hers. 'And I get that it was hard for you. But that shouldn't stop me from knowing who he is.'

'Fine. But don't say I didn't warn you.'

Friday 11th August

I can't help it. I want to figure Nicholas out. Find out what happened to him. Give myself some kind of explanation as to why he doesn't want me. It's all I've been able to think about all week, which I realise is pathetic, but it has taken my mind off my search for my dad.

So, I've decided to take a half day from work and go up to Peterborough with Alice and Erica. Erica's meeting Jack's daughter Esme, from his previous relationship, for the first time so she kind of needs the support. And if I get a chance to find out a little more about Nicholas then great. I'm a glutton for punishment it seems.

Peterborough is... well, its bloody different to Brighton. The main thing I've noticed is that there seems to be A roads to bloody everywhere! Nothing seems within walking distance. We got a budget room in one of those cheap hotels. More like a motel really, but it's something. Jack did offer to put us up at his parents' house, but he warned there wasn't much room and I prefer to have our own space, anyway.

'This is it,' Erica declares, looking at room number 232. The three is hanging off, upside down.

'Thank God,' Alice wails. 'My feet are killing me.'

I look down at her red polka dot heels. 'Well you did insist on wearing *them*.'

She sticks her tongue out. 'I told you, I'm trying to break them in!'

Erica opens the door and we follow her in. The smell of smoke hits me the minute we walk in. Shit, there must have been a football team smoking in here before us.

'Eugh, it stinks,' Alice whines, hand pegging her nose.

I peg my own. 'Eugh, its gross!' I can't sleep in here.

'Look around,' Erica says with an eye roll. 'The

whole room is appalling.'

There's one double bed with stained white sheets. I dread to think what those stains are. Peeling wallpaper in the corner of the room grabs my attention. It looks like a damp problem and the room itself is so small I immediately feel claustrophobic.

'I cannot stay here,' I state, backing out of the room.

Erica follows me out into the hallway. 'Well I'm staying with Jack's mum and dad anyway, but they don't have much spare space.'

I could always stay with Nicholas. The idea has me smiling devilishly to myself. Calm down Brooke, he doesn't want you. Yet.

Alice is already typing into her phone. 'There doesn't seem to be any available nearby hotels.'

'Oh yeah,' Erica groans, as if a bell has rung in her head, 'there's some kind of food festival on this weekend.'

Trust us to choose the one busy weekend in Peterborough.

'It's fine,' I insist breezily. 'I'm sure one of the boys will put us up.'

'I bloody hope so,' Alice mutters, looking back into the room in disgust. 'There's no way I'm staying in there.'

'Leave it with me,' I wink. 'I'm sure I can persuade them.'

Nicholas

I can't believe she's here in Peterborough. Just knowing I could bump into her any minute has me agitated. I can't help but wonder if she's here to see me. Or even worse, what if she's here to see Tom? Shit has changed now. I can't bear to see them together anymore.

So, when he picks me up on the way to the pub I can't help but want to ask him about her.

'Alright, lad,' he says, a full grin on his face. Charlie's in the back tapping away on his phone. He nods a hello.

I get in, annoyed that Charlie is here. I can't really ask him about Brooke without Charlie ripping the piss out of me.

'Looking forward to seeing the girls?' I ask them as casually as I can.

'Hell yeah!' Tom practically shouts. He seems pumped. He better not try anything with her.

Charlie nods. 'Just a bit gutted Molly's not come.'

Me and Tom roll our eyes.

I turn towards him. 'Dude, she's gay. I keep telling you this.'

He rolls his eyes. 'I know. I keep telling you I only

like her as a friend, but will you fuckers listen? Of course not.'

I turn my attention back to Tom. 'So... you know Brooke's coming up, right?'

'Of course,' he grins with a wink. 'Which means a guaranteed bang for me.'

God, I could growl right now. My body tenses up. Count to ten, count to ten.

He laughs. 'And you could get one if you work on snow queen Alice.'

I turn to him, pissed as fuck. This is so typical Tom.

'What, just because she has tats, I'm supposed to fancy her, right?'

His eyes widen. 'Whoa, chill out, bro. I take it you don't like Alice then?'

'No, I don't.' I cross my arms across my chest. Actually, that sounded harsh. 'I mean, she's a nice girl, but I don't like her like *that*, is all.'

'Okay, looks like you'll be chilling with Charlie then.' He chuckles.

I want to pound him so hard in the face.

Chapter 8

Friday 11th August Continued

Brooke

We've spent the day shopping. Who knew there was a shopping centre here! I suppose I just kind of assumed it would be a small village or something but they have everything we have. I guess that's why I failed geography.

But I can't help but be edgy as we walk into what I'm told is their local pub. I'm dressed in dark jeans with a red top which shows off my cleavage amazingly, if I do say so myself. My heels match it perfectly and I have a slick of matching lipstick on my lips.

I look hot. Ready to show Nicholas what he's missing.

I spot him straight away. Sat down with Tom and Charlie, drinking a Peroni. God, how I'd love to be that bottle against his lips. Shit. Have things got that bad? Pull yourself together Brooke. Must stop drooling.

I head to sit next to Nicholas but Tom pulls out the chair next to him, jumping up.

'M'lady,' he jokes with a dramatic bow.

Well, I can't exactly ignore it now, can I? Plus, maybe I want to make Nicholas jealous. Show him what he turned down.

God, I'm turning into a teenager around him. How pathetic. I can't believe I pitied Erica on Luna Island. I'm turning into her.

When I look up, I see Nicholas glaring at me with such abhorrence it almost penetrates my chest. What the hell is his problem? I've only sat next to the guy. I'm hardly giving him a lap dance.

'So, Brooke, Jack was saying your hotels a shit hole. Fancy staying round mine tonight?' Tom asks me with a cheeky wink.

I can't help but laugh, he's so bloody shameless. I chance a quick look at Nicholas and his jaw is clenched, awaiting my answer.

'We'll see, won't we,' I answer vaguely with a raise of my eyebrows. I mean, I do need to stay *somewhere.*

God, the atmosphere is awful, but Tom seems completely unaware. I need to escape it.

'I'll get the drinks in,' I offer standing up and

walking to the bar.

As I wait to be served, I overhear a woman next to me talking to her friend.

'No, I think she's here with Tom.'

Wait, are they talking about me?

She suddenly turns towards me. She's got long blonde hair, a pierced nose and killer cheekbones. This bitch could be a model. Who is she and what is she about to say?

'Hiya, sorry to be really random, but are you here with Nicholas?'

Why the hell does she want to know? Who is she to him?

Wait, think rationally, Brooke. This could be my chance to find out more about him. And I suppose I am here with him, among other people and I don't have to be specific.

'Yeah, I am. Why?'

She chews on her lip. 'Oh. Just... please be careful.'

'Be careful?' I repeat with a frown. 'What, are you telling me he's a murderer or something?' I laugh nervously.

Does she actually know him at all? Or is this poor bitch scared of him because of all his tats and those intense eyes. I could understand the misconception.

'No, but I did go out with him for six months a few

years back and he was...' She twists her hands in front of her, clearly uncomfortable.

'He was...?' I ask encouraging her to tell me.

She looks over towards him. He's staring at both of us, his face like thunder. Did I just notice him gulp? Is he nervous at what she's telling me? That means it could be true.

She takes a deep breath as if collecting up her courage. 'He was controlling and possessive. Always accusing me of cheating on him. He has issues. Only I thought you should know before anything develops.'

Jesus, she's telling me I fancy a psychopath? I knew I had questionable taste, but this is ridiculous.

'Sorry, but I just wanted to tell you before I leave.'

I nod, speechless. I've never been speechless before. Ever.

She grabs her bag and hurriedly walks out with her friend, Nicholas shooting daggers towards her the entire time. Well, what the hell was that all about?

Nicholas

Fucking Kerrie. What the fuck has she said to Brooke? Filling her head with lies no doubt. Why couldn't she mind her own business?

Brooke walks back to the table not saying a word. She definitely said something bad about me. Spreading her usual lies no doubt.

She looks at me, a question in her eyes, before quickly looking away. She wants to ask me something. I know she does. I keep trying to catch her eye but she's ignoring me now, turning her attention to the others, most pointedly, Tom.

As the evening goes on Tom becomes more flirtatious with her. It starts with some secret smiles, but quickly turns into him touching her arm every time he laughs. Which is far too much for my liking. Whenever he does something I find her looking at me to check my reaction. I think I've been good at keeping my face impassive so far, but the rage inside me is building.

Only then it goes too far. He places his hand on her thigh. She looks down at it in astonishment, her eyes burning with confusion.

I see red. I can't help it. Then I growl. Loudly.

Everyone turns to look at me. Shit.

'You alright there, mate?' Charlie asks with a grin.

My breathing is so laboured, I can feel the rage burning through my veins causing my muscles to quiver in its wake.

'Stop. Fucking. Touching. Her.' I've said it before I can think. Before I can take it back.

Tom's eyes widen, and he holds his palms up in surrender immediately. 'Whoa, Nic! Who pissed in your cornflakes?'

God, I hate that expression. Everyone's staring at me as if I've grown another head. It doesn't matter. I've gone past the point of caring.

Brooke leans over the table, her face like thunder. 'He can touch me however he likes. Just like *anyone* can touch me however they like. Anyone that wants to. That wants me. You expressed quite clearly that it doesn't include you.'

'Huh?' I glare back at her.

Tom's looking between us, his eyes darting helplessly from side to side.

'You can't brush me off and then be jealous!' she snarls. 'But from all accounts I hear you're a crazy, jealous bastard.'

I sigh. Fucking Kerrie.

'Maybe I am.' That's one of the reasons I'm trying to stay away from her.

She scoffs, crossing her arms. 'Well then it looks like I had a lucky escape,' she glares back.

That hurts.

'Wait,' Tom says, blinking, still dazed, looking between us. 'You two?'

'Nothing happened,' we both say at the same time,

never allowing our eyes to move from glaring at each other.

Tom turns to Brooke. 'But you *wanted* it to?' He almost seems hurt. The obnoxious prick.

She scorns. 'Like you can talk! You're banging any girl that comes across your path. *Including* when you come down to visit me.'

I glower back at her. 'Don't allow him to use you again.'

She almost jumps across the table, pointing her finger at me. 'Fuck you, Nicholas!' She grabs her bag and storms out of the pub.

Well, that couldn't have gone worse.

Brooke

I can't fucking believe that prick. Growling like some fucking animal at everyone and then having the cheek to tell Tom not to touch me. Newsflash, I'm not his. He said himself he doesn't want me, told me to stay away from him. I'm bloody trying to do that but the controlling prick doesn't want me to have anyone else either. Typical.

I stormed out of that pub so quickly without consideration of where the hell I was going. It's not like

I could go back to the hotel. It's a fucking dive and I'll probably be murdered in my sleep. Damn it.

'Brooke, wait!'

I turn around to see not Tom or the girls following me, but Nicholas. Crazy fucking Nicholas.

I give him the finger and continue on walking. It would help if I had any fucking idea of where I'm going. This place is just like an A road maze!

'I said wait, woman!' he snaps, grabbing my arm and forcing me back to look at him. Shit, he's a fast runner. It must be those lean, long legs. No Brooke, don't get distracted.

'Get your hands off me, psychopath!' I yell, wrenching my arm from him. Shit, it's sore.

His eyes flare, anger emitting off them so strong I look away, scared they'll physically hurt me.

'I'm sorry, okay?' he shouts begrudgingly.

I look back up at him, unsure whether I've heard him right. He's sorry? He's actually apologising?

'Too right you should be sorry. Nobody and I mean *nobody* owns me and I have every right to flirt with anyone I choose.'

His eyes bore into mine. 'That's where you're wrong, Brooke. I own you, you just don't realise it yet.'

I feel my anger reach boiling point. 'Sorry, are you slow or something? You said yourself that you don't want me. I basically offered myself to you and you knocked me back. What part of that makes you think you own me?'

He sighs heavily, dragging his hand through his hair. 'Brooke, I never said I didn't want you. I said that it was best you stayed away from me. That I'm not good for you.'

I roll my eyes. 'Yeah, yeah, so you keep saying. Why?'

He sighs again, shaking his head. 'I... I guess I'm complicated.'

'Or are you totally fucked up?' I retort cruelly. 'Your ex-girlfriend has a lot to say about you. Told me you were a controlling, possessive freak. And from what I've seen so far I have to say I'd agree with her.'

He looks crestfallen. Oh God, I've gone too far. What the hell is wrong with me? The guy is clearly a little bit broken and now I've gone and pushed him off the edge.

'You're right,' he admits quietly.

'No, I'm not. I'm sorry, I didn't mean that,' I apologise quickly, wanting nothing more than to throw myself into his arms and beg his forgiveness.

'No, you're right,' he insists with a nod. 'She's right. That's why I'm warning you off. Just because I don't want you messed around by Tom doesn't mean I want to put you through the head fuck that is me.'

He's admitting he's a possessive control freak? Wow, this is new. I'm not used to guys admitting anything. Ever.

I scrunch my eyes shut. I can't deal with this right now, I just want my bed. And then I remember that awful place where we're staying.

'Do you know the way to Jack's house?' I ask him, attempting to depart from this conversation.

'Yeah, obviously. Why?' He narrows his eyes on me.

'I'm gonna have to ask his parents if I can stay. There's no way I'm staying at that shitty hotel.'

He takes my hand and starts pulling me along after him. Where the hell is he taking me? I struggle against him, but quickly realise there's no point. God, he's a stubborn bastard.

'Where are you taking me?'

'You're coming back to mine.'

I stop dead in my tracks, enough to shock him into turning towards me. 'What? I hope to God you don't think I'm going to sleep with you.'

He rolls his eyes. 'No, dickhead. You're sleeping in my spare room.'

'Oh.'

Why do I sound disappointed? That's very gentlemanly of him. To be fair, when I think back, a lot of what he does is much like a gentleman. Well, a crazy possessive alpha gentleman at least.

He slows down, finally, outside a small three bed semi. You can tell it hasn't been updated properly in years, with the neighbours sporting fully opened up drives and flashy lighting. There's still only space for one car with a small lawn next to it and the lighting seems to be from the original eighties. Yet it's still very smart looking. The grass is freshly mown and the windows sparkling.

He turns to face me, taking me by my shoulders. 'Now, the thing with my dad.'

His dad? Why is he feeling the need to warn me about him?

'He's a bit lonely and doesn't get out much so I'm gonna have to check in with him first.'

'Ri-ight? So, can't I come meet him too? Or does he have two heads or something?'

He frowns. 'You can meet him, but he'll only get stupid ideas into his head. He's got ridiculous notions about relationships.'

'Like what?' I frown.

'Like that people can live happily ever after.'

Wow, he's more broken than I thought. Not that I don't agree with him.

His face becomes pained. I stare at him, my mind spinning in confusion.

'What about your mum? What's she like?'

His arms tense, his face turning rigid. 'Don't bring her up.'

He grabs my hand and drags me in before I have a chance to register it. His parents aren't together? No-one mentioned that to me. Way to put your foot in it Brooke.

'Hi, Dad,' he calls as soon as we're inside the small hallway wallpapered in lavender tones. He smiles fretfully at me before pulling me down the hall to the sitting room.

His dad sits in a green leather chair holding a can of Carlsberg, watching football. He turns in his chair.

'So how was the pub?' he asks with an eager smile. He spots me and quickly straightens up, putting his beer down. 'Oh, hello. Sorry I didn't know we were expecting anyone.'

'Dad, this is my friend Brooke.'

I snort internally. Friend. We're not friends. God knows what we are, but it's definitely not friends. More than friends, but less than lovers.

He jumps up and offers his hand, his chubby cheeks rising into a friendly smile.

'So lovely to meet you, Brooke.'

I return his handshake and give what I hope is a friendly smile. How on earth is his dad so welcoming when his son is an emotionally unstable nutcase?

'Brooke's staying the night. Her hotel is a bit of a dive.'

'You're not staying at that Premier Lodge, are you?' His dad asks with a comical grin.

'Actually... yes,' I admit.

'Oh,' he grimaces. Jeez, you'd think the guys would have warned us.

'Yeah,' Nicholas grins. 'You girls should have asked our opinion first. That place is known as a dive around here.' Him and his dad exchange a smile. 'Anyway, we're headed up to bed.'

His dad notices him taking my hand before I'm basically dragged up the stairs and to a room at the end of the creaky beige corridor.

His room is not what I expected. It's pristine, with barely anything out of place. His black and white bedspread is made to perfection. Was he in the army or something?

He grabs a t-shirt out of his top drawer as I notice the framed Marvel comics hung along one wall. 'Here, you can sleep in this. I'll show you the spare room.'

Is it me or has he suddenly turned cold towards me?

I follow him to the other end of the corridor where I'm presented with a beige room, with a brown bedspread over a single bed, a plastic single flower on the bedside table. Hardly homely, but for two guys it's surprisingly nice.

'Thanks.' I look up to him, feeling ridiculously close in this small room.

He's glaring down at me. Wait, is that glaring or something else? Is it hunger in his eyes? His breathing has accelerated, his chest rising and falling dramatically, as if he's going to burst out of his t-shirt.

In that very moment, I want him more than I've ever wanted anyone, every cell in my body wants to reach out and touch him. But the fear of rejection is still so fresh in my mind, holding me back.

But... Oh, fuck it.

Before I can reason with myself I've closed the small distance between us, gone on my tiptoes and planted a soft kiss on his lips. I hover a millimetre away from them, giving him the chance to reciprocate.

A couple of seconds pass. Wow. So, this is what rejection feels like. It stings.

I open my eyes, ready to make some kind of awkward joke, when I'm suddenly grabbed around the head and his hot lips are smashing against mine. Fuck.

I place my arms out to steady myself, but there's no need. He's wrapping my body into his, while his arms encase me. I fit perfectly.

His tongue teases at my pursed lips. I open up,

eager for the kiss to deepen, my body tingling with anticipation. He plunges his tongue in, greedily claiming my mouth. My tongue tangles with his, groaning at the feeling that travels from my head all the way down my spine.

Then he's pulling away all too soon. He still has hold of my face as he looks down at me, his mouth open and gasping for breath. I get a rush knowing I caused that.

He releases his hands from my face. I almost whimper from the loss of contact. His warm hands on my face feel needed all of a sudden, as essential as oxygen.

'I'm sorry,' he utters with a frown. He quickly turns and walks away.

Where the hell is he going? It was just getting good!

'I'm not,' I shout after him, just before his bedroom door slams itself shut.

Well, fuck. He gets more baffling by the second.

Chapter 9

Saturday 12th August

Okay, fuck this. Three hours I've been tossing and turning, unable to sleep knowing he's just down the corridor. I can still feel the tingling sensation in my skin as he touched me. I can still taste his kisses, smell his luscious aftershave. Just remembering it has me horny as fuck.

Especially with him leaving me like that straight after. I mean, what is he? A sadistic bastard? Showing me what I can't have? It's a sick form of punishment in my book.

I feel like I need to pace and it's not like I can just get up and about. I'm in a stranger's house. What if I were to bump into his dad? How mortifying. But God, the need to see Nicholas is as if he has his very own magnet pulling me towards him. Just so I can see if he's half as affected as me.

Fuck it, I'm doing it.

I tiptoe up to the door and open it, peering out into the dark hallway. I haven't heard his dad go to bed and I can still hear the TV on downstairs so I'm hoping that means he's passed out in front of it and has less chance of catching me sneaking around like a slut.

Next, I tiptoe down the hallway, each footstep creaking louder than the last. I wince each time, hoping to God I don't wake his dad.

I make it to the door and raise my hand, wondering if I should knock first. That's assuming he's asleep. It's 2am. He's probably been asleep since his head hit the pillow. Not a horny mess like me.

No, I shouldn't knock. I'll just have a peep in and see if he's awake. I carefully open the door, the slight sliver of light shining into his room. It lights up his face and naked chest spread across the bed. He stretches, his tired eyes open and looking at me.

'Hey,' he says, his voice croaky. 'You okay?'

Oh God, he *was* sleeping. He doesn't give a shit. He's just being nice.

'Yeah,' I whisper back. 'I was just... checking to see if you were awake. I can't get to sleep.'

He waves me in. 'Come here.'

I waver, not wanting to intrude on his cosiness.

He yanks back the cover, studying my face with

curious eyes, obviously wondering why I'm still standing here.

Okay. Here we go.

I practically run towards him, slamming the door behind me and diving under the warm covers. He wraps the duvet back around me, wedging it behind my hip so I'm all tucked in.

'Thanks, Mum,' I snort. I'm desperate for something to break the ice.

I turn towards him, the urge to snuggle into the gap under his arm so strong I physically have to restrain myself. The heat that's emanating from his body is just so tempting.

I'm desperate to ask him about his mum. Where she is and what she's doing but I have a feeling he doesn't want to talk about it. He's not very forthcoming with anything.

I pretend to sleepily snuggle into him, losing what ounce of dignity I had. His body freezes for a split second, before he sighs, as if giving into it. He wraps his arm around me, pulling me further into his chest. I put my face into the crook of his neck. He smells bloody amazing. All lemon, sandalwood and musk.

It's divine and drives me wild. God, I ache to taste those lips again.

I move my hands around so my palm strokes his

thigh. He tenses, but doesn't remove it so I continue around to his dick. I find it semi hard and give it a big squeeze. He practically jumps out of his skin.

'Brooke,' he growls. He takes my hand and removes it.

Ouch. The rejection is hard to bear, my cheeks so red I'm glad it's dark. God, why does he not want me? Is he gay?

'What?' I laugh a little to try to lighten the mood.

'You don't need to have sex with me just so you can sleep in my bed.'

I react as if he's slapped me. Does he really think that's what this is? I pull away and sit up in bed.

'That's not what that was,' I bark, my voice ridiculously breaking slightly.

He sighs, a whole lot of frustration in it. 'I'm sorry. Come here.'

I look down at him. He's reaching out to me with a forlorn look on his face. God, he's a good looking specimen.

'No, it's fine.' I swing my legs off the bed. 'I'll go back to the spare room.'

One foot has barely touched the floor before he's grabbed me round the waist and thrown me back on the bed. Whoa. He crawls above me, his arms on either side of my head.

'How many fucking times do I have to tell you?' he growls. 'Of course, I want you to touch my dick, but I'm not allowing it. I don't do relationships anymore.'

I scoff. 'Who said anything about a relationship?' He's seriously talking to the wrong girl.

I reach my hand up to touch his cheek, but he leans on one of his hips, grabbing my hand again. This time more roughly.

'I'm not having sex with you, Brooke. I know once I've done that there will be no going back.' His eyes sparkle with sincerity.

'What do you mean, no going back?'

'I mean you'll be mine. And I don't share what's mine.'

I stare back at him, the intensity behind his eyes drawing me in. There's something behind them. Some sort of fear, of vulnerability.

'So, you either sleep or I'll go into the spare room myself,' he warns.

'No!' I shout far too eagerly. 'Can we just *sleep* together?' God, I sound ridiculous.

He smiles, humour curving the edges of his mouth. 'As long as you actually mean sleeping, then yes.'

He falls onto the mattress behind me, grabbing me around the stomach and snuggling against me, his chin resting on the top of my head. I can't help but grin to myself as his now fully erect dick is pushing against my arse. I wiggle slightly against it.

'Brooke,' he warns slowly.

'Fine, fine. I'll sleep.'

Saturday 12th August continued

I wake ensconced in his arms. His beautiful tattooed arms. I take my time to look over them.

There's a tiger on his left hand with *hate* written on his knuckles. On the thumbs of both hands is half of a beautiful butterfly's wings. I know that if you were to place them together, you'd make a full butterfly. Actually, if he were to do that, then the number thirteen would also be underneath it. I wonder why the number thirteen?

On his right hand, there's a moth or maybe another butterfly. *Love* is written on this hand's knuckles. On his wrist is written *Don't Panic.* Does he suffer from anxiety?

Up his right arm are more roses, black and red; along with a paw print that on closer inspection has a picture of a dog in it. Wow, that's cool. Intricate through the roses is a circle that says *What Goes Around Comes Back Around.* So, he believes in karma. Then it's surrounded by loads of Aztec style patterns, like he got bored while he had a sharpie.

On his left arm is a huge drawing of a misty forest. I can't see the rest without moving from his chest and I don't want to risk waking him. Plus, it might be the most comfortable place in the world.

I really want to see his face though, study it at my leisure without him realising how obsessed with him I am.

I move ever so slowly in his arms, being careful not to wake him, tilting my head to take in his beautiful sleeping form. Wow, he's beautiful up close like this. His dark eyelashes are fanned out showing off how long they are. His skin is pale but flawless, not a single spot or blackhead in sight. I wonder what face wash he uses. And he has the most perfect nose I've ever seen. Is it weird to find a nose attractive? Probably.

His neck has a skull wearing a top hat and a monocle with a few roses underneath it. There's a record player on the back of his neck going around the side. Above that is a Mandala boho tattoo all the way up to the side of his shaved head.

I reach out and touch his perfectly pouted pink lips. I still can't believe they were on mine last night. I almost feel worse for it. Seeing what I can't have. My God, it had been good. If that's how good a kiss felt, imagine sex. I bet he's fucking amazing.

He stirs, his eyes frowning before flickering open and finding me gawking at him. Oops. Well, I look crazy.

His arms leave me to reach over his head in an adorable stretch, his face scrunching up like a bulldog puppy. God, he's sexy as sin.

'Morning,' he says on an intake of a yawn. He's delectable. I want to shower him in kisses, but you know, I'd look mental.

God, I bet I look hideous. I wasn't able to take my make-up off last night so I know I have panda eyes at the very least. Worst case it's gone deep into my pores and I've woken with a big fresh red spot on my chin. I really hope to God I don't have something hideous, like a whitehead. Although as he looks down at me still on his chest, he doesn't seem repulsed.

'Morning,' I smile back, wanting to fully crawl onto his chest and straddle him, but restraining myself. 'I was just looking at your tattoos. How many do you have?'

'I've lost count,' he says, as if it's no big deal.

'What does the thirteen stand for?'

He furrows his eyebrows at me, rubbing sleep out of his eyes. 'Huh?'

I point to his hands. 'The thirteen on your hands.'

'Oh. It's the day Esme was born on.'

And... my womb has exploded. He got a tattoo to

signify Esme's birthday. That is beyond sweet.

'And this one.' I point towards the *Don't Panic.*

He shifts uncomfortably underneath me. 'Just a reminder,' he says, almost on a whisper.

Something tells me he doesn't want me prying into them all. Time to change the subject, Brooke.

'So be honest. How bad is my face this morning?'

His eyes search over me, attempting to hide a grin. 'You look the same.'

'Really?' I ask incredulously.

He bursts out laughing, clutching at his sides, his whole chest vibrating underneath me. 'Of course, you don't,' he chuckles. 'You look like a sleep deprived panda. But luckily for you I think pandas are cute.'

He thinks I'm cute? I can't help but feel my cheeks heat. He holds his stare with mine, a mix of fondness and desire sweeping through them. What is happening to me? I need to get out of here and get my head straight.

'Well, on that note, I should go.' I sit up in bed and run a hand through my knotty hair.

He takes my hand, halting my steps. God, it feels good in his.

'Are you going to the food festival later?'

'Oh yeah, Jack said something about it. I suppose we could pop in before we go.' I wink. God, why am I winking?

He rubs my fingers with his thumb. 'You should. It'll be fun.'

Okay, mind made up.

I meet up with Alice back at the disgusting hotel.

'Do we really need to go to this food festival? Isn't it just going to be a load of lard arses stuffing their faces?' Alice asks with an eye roll.

'Nah, I reckon it'll be a laugh,' I insist as casually as I can. 'Plus, they probably have loads of vegetarian stalls,' I add tempting her.

She eyes me up knowingly, arms crossed over her chest. 'You only want to go because Nicholas will be there.'

'No, I don't!' I retort like a bloody teenager. Way to play it cool, Brooke. Way to play it cool.

She chuckles, while smiling smugly. 'What the hell is going on between you two, anyway? Did you sleep with him last night?'

Apparently, she crashed on Jack's sofa. And wondered if I was shagging Nicholas.

My cheeks start to blush at just the memory of his half naked body pressed up against me, warming me through.

'Well, *officially* we slept together.'

'No!' she shrieks, her grin wide. 'You ho bag.' I know she's saying it with love.

I chuckle. 'No, it was weird. We actually slept. No sex.'

'No nookie?' she asks, startled. Her eyes are practically popping out of her head.

'No nookie,' I nod in confirmation.

'So, are you not into him or something?' She starts lining her lips with her dark red shade. 'I could have sworn I felt some sexy vibes being shot out of your vag towards him.'

I double over laughing. 'You've been hanging around with me for too long! You never used to speak like this.'

She snorts a laugh. 'So, what's the problem? Why didn't you bang?'

I sigh, suddenly feeling ridiculously deflated. 'It seems he doesn't bang. He's a relationship guy, and from his warnings and that of his ex, I think I'm having a lucky escape. He's one intense fucker.'

She shrugs. 'So, what's the big deal? You don't do relationships, so just cut your losses.'

I throw myself down on the bed. 'I bloody wish I could, but it's like he's telling me to back off while pulling me in.'

She mulls it over a second. 'So maybe you break

your no relationship rule and give him a chance?'

I roll my eyes. 'I don't think so.' The last thing I want is to turn into my mother, obsessed over one man. 'But... God, we did kiss, and it was...' I find myself touching my lips at the memory of his plump ones on mine.

She raises her eyebrows, an amused grin on her face. 'I'm taking it he's a good kisser?'

I groan. 'The best. Like, he should win an award or something.'

She sighs loudly. 'Damn, I haven't had a kiss like that for years.'

I sigh too, like a swoony girl. 'Anyway, Erica's meeting us there, right?'

I know she's been ridiculously nervous about meeting Esme and Amber. The first time meeting Jack's daughter is kind of a big deal.

'Yep. I can't wait to hear how it goes.' She links arms with me. 'Until then let's go stuff our faces like fat bitches.'

'Let's do it.'

'But do me a favour and don't leave me with Tom "Manwhore" Maddens again. That guy is seriously too much.'

Chapter 10

Saturday 12th August Continued

An hour later we're arriving at the manor house that the festival is taking place at. Live folk music blasts out of speakers; while the lawn is covered in different coloured stalls boasting hot food, real ale and wine. We spot the guys from across the lawn that's littered with children running around with bubble guns. I wave—a little too eagerly in hindsight.

Tom saunters over. 'Hey, you girls made it.' He grabs both of us into a hug.

'Ugh!' Alice practically screams. 'Tom, did you just grab my arse?'

'Guilty!' he grins, holding up his hands. There's not a hint of an apology.

She contorts her face in disgust. 'You are *such* a pig!'

'Oink, oink, baby.' He grins and winks. I can feel the anger radiating from her.

Nicholas hovers nearby with his hands in his jacket pocket as Charlie walks over and hugs us hello. God, he's so sexy in a whole geeky, awkward kind of way.

'Right,' I say with a clap of my hands. 'Where to first?'

'The wine tent?' Alice says with an eye roll. 'Obviously.'

We start walking, Nicholas trailing behind us. Why is he being so weird? Is he regretting letting me sleep in his bed?

We arrive at the tent decorated with gaudy plastic grapes. Myself, Alice and Charlie have a cool, crisp glass of fruity wine. Shame it's in a plastic cup, but beggars can't be choosers.

Next, the boys take us to the beer tent where they sample different ales before deciding on one called Red Nose Randall. Sounds a bit Christmassy to me, but they seem to like it.

'Right,' Tom says with a clap. 'Where to next?'

'I think we should split up,' Nicholas requests out of nowhere.

We all turn to look at him, hands still in his pockets as he leans against the bar. It's the first thing he's said all afternoon.

'Why?' Charlie asks, his forehead creased with a frown.

Nicholas takes my hand and starts pulling me towards him. 'I want to show Brooke around.'

Wow, possessive much? What's going on with him? He ignores me the whole time and now wants me all to himself?

I look back at the others to see Tom's eyes widen before a knowing grin settles on his face. 'Okay, Lothario. You guys do that and we'll show ice queen around.' He wraps his arm around Alice's neck yanking her to him and ruffling her hair.

'What the fuck, Maddens!' she screams. 'It took me ages to do this hair.' She shoves him off, getting her pocket mirror out to try to fix it. Tom rolls his eyes.

'Don't worry,' Charlie says, noticing my concern. 'I'll make sure they don't kill each other.'

'Thanks, Charlie.' I rip myself out of Nicholas' grip to give him a quick hug, pressing my boobs against him in thanks.

Nicholas takes my hand again and greedily pulls me back so he's pressed against my back. He growls ever so quietly in my ear. It makes me almost choke on nothing but air.

'Okay, see you later,' I wave, turning to follow Nicholas who's dragging me off like an impatient child wanting to see Santa.

We walk side by side in silence. 'So... I take it you're

a bit shit at small talk?'

He grins briefly, putting his hand through his hair. 'I just don't see the point in talking unless you've got something to say.'

'That's deep, bro,' I mock, putting on a douche guy voice.

He rolls his eyes, attempting to hide the grin trying to curl the corner of his mouth. I don't know why he fights enjoying himself.

'So where exactly are we going?'

He interlocks our fingers. 'I want to show you my mate's stall. He does Thai street food.'

I grimace. I've always hated Thai food. 'Sounds gross.'

He rolls his eyes. 'It's not cooked on the pavement. Trust me, you'll love it.'

Do I trust him? God, the weird thing is that I do. I feel safe with him, safe in the knowledge that he'll look after me. It's probably the safest I've ever felt. I've never had a man in my life to rely on, but something deep within tells me that this guy would drop everything to be by my side.

But do I want to jump head first into a relationship with a self-professed crazy? Hardly the ideal first relationship for a commitment-phobe like me.

After what feels like forever walking, we stop in

front of a turquoise coloured food truck. A Thai guy in his late twenties is serving food to a long queue of people. Well, they're busy. That must be a good sign. We join them at the end of the line.

'So, they must be good, if people are queuing?' I ask him, desperate for some conversation. It feels so strange that only last night we were sharing a bed and now I'm feeling awkward around him.

'This is nothing. We've caught him at a quiet moment. Trust me, his food is amazing.' It's the most passionate I've ever seen him.

I wonder if now I've got him stuck with me I can get away with quizzing him a bit more about his life.

'So... your mum. She doesn't live with you?' I ask, trying to sound as breezy as possible.

'No,' is his flat answer. Well, this is like pulling teeth.

'Oh.' I rock on my heels. 'Does she live nearby?' I press.

A sudden sadness crosses over his face. Oh shit. She's dead, isn't she? Of course she is and doughnut here just brings it up to upset him while he's in public.

'I'm so sorry. Has she passed?' I ask, putting my hand on his bicep. Wow, it's strong. I give it a little squeeze.

He frowns. 'No, she's still alive. Well, I think she is.'

'Oh?'

He sighs heavily as if the weight of the world is on his shoulders. 'She left when I was seven.' His eyes stoop down to the floor, before peering back up at me, curious for my reaction.

She left him? I imagine a little seven-year-old Nicholas, tall and skinny for his age. Now I imagine him abandoned by the one woman who should love him more than anything in the world. God, what the hell would have happened for her to leave him so callously? My mother might have been shit, but at least she stuck around.

'I'm so sorry.' I rub his back. His long, lean back. No, don't get distracted Brooke! 'Does she stay in touch?'

He shakes his head. 'No. I haven't seen or heard from her since she went.'

'So why did she go? What the hell happened for her to just abandon her son?' I'm actually shocked at how angry I am over this, but what a bitch!

He shakes his head. 'No big reason. Dad said she wanted to be free again.'

'What a bitch,' I blurt out. 'Shit, sorry. I know that's still your mum.'

'It's cool,' he says with a shrug.

'I'm looking for my dad right now,' I blurt out, in a desperate bid to make him feel better. For him to feel I understand.

'Really?' he asks, a line appearing between his brows. 'When did he leave?'

'Well, he was actually gone before I was born. My mum's a bit of a nightmare. I really can't blame him.'

His long lashes flutter before his eyes narrows at me. 'Does he even know you exist?'

'Yep.' I shrug. 'I found her diary. He wanted me aborted.'

'Wow. Harsh.'

'My mum will never talk about it. I'm always trying to squeeze information out of her, but now I've got a detective on it.'

'You're joking?' he snorts. 'You're paying one of those crooks?'

I balk. 'They're not all crooks!'

He leans on one hip, raising his eyebrows. 'Well I could get you any information you needed, anyway.'

I look up at him, bewildered. 'Why? Are you Inspector Gadget in your spare time or something?' I laugh at my own joke. Sometimes I'm hilarious.

He lowers his eyes at me. 'No, *obviously*. But everyone has a digital footprint. I could find him online if you give me his name.'

'Well, that's the thing. I only have a photo and a first name.'

'Ah. Slightly trickier,' he agrees just as we get to the front of the queue.

'Nic!' the young Thai guy says in excitement. 'Good to see you, man!' His eyes travel over to me. 'And who is this pretty lady?'

I snort at being called a lady. It's so rare these days.

'This is Brooke,' he says proudly, puffing out his chest.

I awkwardly wave.

'You his new lady?' he asks with a cheeky wink.

Uh-oh. Way to spread the awkward.

'No, I'm a single lady,' I announce, taking away the awkward question from Nicholas. I actually flash my bare wedding finger and jokingly do the Beyoncé *Single Ladies* dance.

Nicholas bursts out laughing. Way to make a dick out of yourself, Brooke.

'Right, the usual for you, Nic?' he asks him.

'Not today,' he answers with a shake of his head. 'I want to get a few different things so I can show you off to Brooke. Try to impress her.'

'Ah, I'm with you, my man.'

'I'll have...'

He reels off a load of Thai food, half of which I've never heard of before. We're handed over a large tray with cardboard containers and some plastic cutlery.

'Enjoy, guys,' he says with a wink. He sure does like to wink.

'We will,' Nicholas nods with a smile. I don't think I've ever seen him so happy. Note to self: Thai street food makes him happy.

We find an empty hay bale and sit ourselves down. He starts unpacking the food, opening up the containers and giving them a sniff, like he's a heroin addict or something.

He must notice my dubious face. 'Trust me. It's delicious. Just close your eyes and I'll feed you something.'

Ugh, I hate when people try to feed me.

'Feed me something? I'm not a toddler you know.'

His lips flatten. 'Just relinquish control for once, will you?'

What's he trying to say? That I'm a control freak? Hey, I'm easy bloody breezy.

I squeeze my eyes shut and open my mouth. 'If you stick your dick in I'll bite,' I warn, my lips in a tight smile.

He chuckles. God it's a beautiful sound.

I open my mouth tentatively and wait for some food. A small portion of something is softly placed in my mouth. I give it a chew and oh my God, it's the most beautiful chicken I've ever eaten, in a peanut sauce I've never tasted before.

'That is amazing,' I admit, opening my eyes to find him looking at me with such admiration in those midnight blues I almost collapse. I grin like a big stupid girl.

I look away and instead spot a familiar face. Where do I know that guy from? He's watching me so he must know me too. I go to raise my hand to wave, but he disappears as quickly as I've spotted him. It's the same guy from the Proud parade. What the hell is he doing here, in Peterborough, watching me again. Is he some kind of weird stalker or something? I laugh at my own over-dramatics.

I instead focus on the delicious food and willingly help myself to the rest, stuffing my face. Luckily, he's only got sample portions of everything otherwise I'd be stuffed and have to be rolled home.

'Right, ready for another wander?' he asks, taking my hand as he dumps the tray contents in a bin.

'Yep.'

As I stand up, he takes my hand from his and instead drapes his arm around my shoulders. My God, why is it I feel so swoony around him?

We walk for a little while in comfortable silence. It's funny how I'm quickly getting used to the companionable silences.

After a while I spot a sign that says 'Man vs Food.'

'What's that?'

He laughs, squeezing me closer to him. 'Oh, this stupid competition where you have to eat the most. Me and the boys did it last year.'

'Really?' I chuckle. 'Who won?'

He looks down bashfully as if embarrassed. 'Me.'

'What?' I stop walking and turn to him, bemused. '*You* won that thing? Are you an ex fatty or something?'

He laughs, his cheeks turning the slightest shade of pink. 'Nah, but yeah, I can eat,' he nods.

'Do any women ever enter?' I'm sure all the entrants must be pussies if he was the bloody winner. It's not like he's known as an eater.

He shakes his head. 'Nah. I think the name Men vs Food puts them off.'

The feminist in me rises, angry as fuck.

'Well that's ridiculously sexist.'

He quirks an eyebrow up. 'To be fair, I don't think girls can eat like us guys.'

I scoff. 'You've got to be kidding, right? I can eat for England.'

'What, even after all that Thai food?'

I snort. 'No problem.'

He grabs an application form, thrusting it at my chest. 'Prove it.'

So that's how I've found myself standing next to Nicholas behind a long table with other guys eager to win this competition. A woman with ridiculously big tits wheels out a tea cart, trays of hotdogs piled high on it. Mmm, my favourite. She starts serving them out to us.

'Luckily for me I love a sausage,' I whisper into Nicholas' ear. I finish it with a wink.

He growls back at me. It drives me wild how jealous he gets. Is it weird that it feels like it's his own way of showing he cares? I must have issues if I find this sexy.

'Right, gents,' the guy with the megaphone shouts. I cough loudly. 'And ladies,' he says with a nod to me. 'Most hotdogs eaten within a minute wins.' With that he blows the whistle.

I waste no time. I grab the hotdog and get stuck in. My theory with this isn't to stuff it all in my mouth, it's taking smaller bites more often. Chew twice, swallow, bite and repeat. I don't let any of my surroundings distract me. I know if I look at Nicholas I'll burst out laughing and I don't have the time to spare.

There's a point to prove here. I have to make a stand for women. Women can eat just as much and as fast as men. We're equals dammit. Especially when it comes to eating hotdogs.

My jaw is already aching and I'm having to take occasional glugs of lemonade to moisten my mouth, the hotdog rolls the hardest to chew down.

The whistle blows when it feels like it's been only twenty seconds.

I swallow down what I've got in my mouth, knowing it's allowed. The man with the megaphone starts going through people's trays and counting. I look to Nicholas. He's grinning at me in a mix of amusement and admiration.

The big boobed woman whispers into the announcer's ear. He nods his head towards her before speaking into his megaphone again.

'And the winner this year, in a shocking turn of events, is our first ever woman applicant, a Miss Brooke Archer.'

I won? I fucking won?

The guy is suddenly at my side raising my hand in the air in victory. The crowd is going wild, cheering me on like I'm some sort of champion. Like I cured cancer or something. Not gobbled down hotdogs like a fat bitch.

'I can't believe you won,' Nicholas shouts with a laugh over the crowd, clapping along too.

I wink and bow my head at my adoring crowd. The guy with the megaphone hands over my prize. It's a voucher for a lifetime supply of hotdogs from the local supermarket. Nice.

'Come on, fatty,' Nicholas snorts, offering me his hand.

I take it and let him lead me off the stage, the crowd still applauding.

'Where the hell did you learn to eat like that?' he asks with a grin.

I'm about to tell him how in our house if you didn't gobble your food down quickly you'd have it stolen from you by Madison, when I suddenly feel nauseous.

The food starts to come back up my throat and before I can help myself I'm arching my back and spewing up over the grass. Oh my god, this *cannot* be happening in front of Nicholas. It just can't.

I fall to my knees, not wanting the vomit to go on my new converse. *This is so humiliating.*

His hands find my hair, pulling it back so I don't vomit into it. God, he's a keeper. Well, at least that's what a normal woman looking for a relationship would think.

It finally slows and I'm able to take some gulps of air. I take the bottle of water passed to me by the big titted lady who I earlier judged. Who knew she was such a sweetheart.

I swish the water around my mouth and then spit it out before taking a few healthy sips.

'You okay now?' he asks, turning me to him.

I nod, unable to meet his eyes, mortified.

'Here,' he says offering me a chewing gum. I take it gratefully, pleased to get the awful taste from my mouth.

'Can we please just pretend like that didn't happen?' I beg with pleading eyes.

'Yep,' he nods, wrapping his hand round my waist and guiding me away from my vomit puddle. 'So, I think I was asking where on earth you learnt to eat like that?'

I smile to myself, pleased he's being so kind to me. 'Trust me, when you have fat evil stepsisters like me, you have to wolf down your food or it'll get taken off your plate. But as you can tell I'm out of practise.'

He studies my face as if trying to read me. 'You have stepsisters?'

I shake my head. 'Well, no. They're actually half-sisters, but I got into my head when I was younger that I was Cinderella and they were my evil stepsisters.'

'Oh yeah,' he smiles. 'Waiting for a prince to save you from your tower, were you?'

I snort. '*Please.* I quickly realised that the only person who was going to save me was myself. I learnt early on not to rely on men and I still don't.'

'Doesn't mean you shouldn't sometimes, though.'

'What do you mean?' I ask, still a bit dazed from the vomiting.

He stops and looks at me intently, his midnight blues boring into me. 'I mean that you should let guys in occasionally. They might surprise you.'

I snort a sarcastic laugh. 'I told you, I'm not a relationship kind of girl.'

He sighs, tucking a bit of hair behind my ear. 'But why? Who hurt you so badly that you never want another one?'

I laugh cruelly. 'Sorry to disappoint you, but there's no big dramatic heartbreak story to tell you. I just grew up watching my mum change everything about herself to please the men that were in her life, only for them to let her down. I don't want that for myself. So, I use men for what I want, end of story. When guys do it they're hailed as heroes. When girls do it we're slags. It's not fair.'

He grins at me as if he finds me hilarious. 'I'm starting to think you're one of those nutty feminists.'

My nostrils flare in rage. 'Yes, I am a fucking feminist. No, I'm not nutty. That's half the problem.' I poke him in the chest with my finger. 'Male chauvinist pigs like you calling us mad for wanting equal rights.'

'Wow,' he snickers, hands up in surrender. 'I didn't mean it like that.'

'I'm sure you didn't. Guys like you never do.' I stomp off, unsure of my next direction.

He runs and stops right in front of me blocking my

path. 'I'm not like that. And I'll prove it to you.'

'Oh yeah?' I challenge, arms crossed against my chest.

'Yep. Come on. I'm taking you to the cake tent.'

'The cake tent? What the hell?'

We make it to a huge tent right as they're announcing the winner of best cake, the most delicious Victoria sponges lined up behind nervous contestants.

'Nigel Parker.'

Why is that surname familiar? Wait, is that his dad walking up to the winner's stand?

'That's your dad!' I gasp in disbelief.

'Yep,' he says while clapping. 'How can I be a sexist pig when I was raised by a man who makes the best Victoria sponge in Peterborough?'

We burst out laughing, so hard I'm sure I'm going to pee myself.

When it's time to say goodbye and be driven back by Charlie I find myself not wanting to leave Nicholas' side. It might as well be different sides of the world for how far Peterborough feels.

'Look after yourself,' he says on a sigh, pulling me into a hug.

I hug him back with as much force as I can before being the one to pull back first. I don't want to look like a crazy clinger.

'Same to you. Remember that I'm not some frilly little girl who needs to look after herself.'

He smiles. 'No, I forgot. You're a strong, independent feminist.'

I wink. 'And don't you forget it.'

When we get back from the festival Erica's already waiting for us in the divey hotel room. If you can even call it a hotel room. I'm dying to find out how she got on meeting Esme and Amber. I smile at her as we walk in, but she's sat on the end of the bed, her shoulders tense. Uh-oh. Did it not go well?

'Hey, babe, what's wrong?'

She frowns, biting her lip. 'Oh God.' She tucks her hair behind her ear with a shaky hand. 'It was awful.'

Oh no! I hate seeing her upset like this.

I put my arm around her shoulder and sit next to her on the bed. Alice sits down on her other side.

'What the fuck happened?' Maybe Esme's a little brat who told her to fuck off. 'Is she a little bitch?'

'No,' she shakes her head, a stray tear trailing down her cheek. 'That's what makes it all so much harder. She's adorable. Fucking adorable. And so inquisitive. You can tell she's going to be really clever.'

Alice leans back to look at me with raised eyebrows.

'So, what's the problem?' Alice asks, like me clearly at a loss.

She sighs, eyes drooped. 'It's her mum, Amber.'

My anger spikes. Do I need to kill her? Because I will. Erica's the nicest fucking person I know and if this bitch is making her life hard, I'll do whatever it takes to protect her.

'What did she say?' I demand.

She sighs, wiping her cheek with the back of her hand. 'Well, we had a play with Esme in the garden and then Amber invited me in for a cup of tea. I thought she was being all friendly.' She scoffs, rolling her eyes. 'How dumb am I?'

'You're not dumb,' I insist, rubbing her back in soothing circles.

'So, once we were settled with tea she told me in no uncertain terms that she didn't want me seeing her daughter.'

'She WHAT?' I bellow, fury taking over my volume control.

'Yep,' she nods, closing her eyes as if it hurts to remember. 'She told me that I was just a phase he was going through, trying to relive his teenage years and that he'd soon move back to Peterborough.'

'What did you say back?' Alice asks, warning me with her eyes to calm down.

'I couldn't even speak! I was in total shock.' She breaks into a light sob. I rub her back again. 'She went on to say that she didn't want Esme to get used to me only for me to disappear in a few months.'

'What a cow.'

'I tried to explain that we were serious, but she told me that unless we were getting married, she didn't want me seeing her.'

God, this bitch sounds awful. Well, I suppose that's why Jack broke up with her in the first place. It's just a shame he didn't realise that before he put a baby inside her.

'Did you tell Jack?' Alice asks.

She sniffs. 'No, of course not.'

'Why bloody not?' I demand. 'He needs to know that his ex is a psycho who's trying to scare you off.'

She shakes her head. 'Ugh, I just don't want to rock the boat. He was so pleased we'd gotten on so well. I don't want to piss all over it.'

I suppose I can understand that. Erica getting along with Esme is a big deal to Jack, understandably.

'Well, you'll need to bring it up sooner or later. What about next time he invites you to go up to see her? You'll have to come up with some lame excuse and he'll assume it's because you're not interested in Esme.'

She frowns. 'God, do you think?'

I shrug. 'It's a possibility.'

'Okay. I'll tell him,' she nods. 'Soon.'

I stare at her warningly. 'Make sure that you do.'

Chapter 11

Tuesday 15th August

I can't believe I miss him. How pathetic is that? It's only been two days but I long for him as if I haven't seen him for weeks. I'm aware I'm being ridiculous, but it's just... ugh, it's just that being so close to him all weekend has given me a taste of what it would be really like to have him. To be with him properly. The damn guy has actually got me considering a relationship.

And it's not like it'd be an easy starter relationship to consider. He's said himself he's a nightmare when he's with someone. I mean, hearing about how his mum left makes me understand why he clearly has such abandonment issues. No wonder he's possessive and clingy.

But is that what I want? Some clingy guy who's going to suffocate me? I don't think so.

The distance is also sure to drive him extra crazy. I

don't think I can cope with that. Not now, not ever.

My phone rings, flashing up with the private detective's number. Shit the bed. Has he found something?

'Hello?' I answer eagerly.

'Miss Archer, it's Detective Maloney.'

Duh, I have caller ID, idiot. God, this is the guy I'm paying to investigate shit?

'Yes. Do you have an update?'

'I have information on your father. Can we meet?'

I'm sitting in the local coffee shop strumming my hands on the table, waiting for this baboon to turn up. Why he couldn't tell me over the phone is beyond me, but he said something about it being sensitive information. I think he just wants me to take him seriously. Loser.

My phone starts ringing in my bag. Damn it, I hope it's not this idiot cancelling. I've just treated myself to a coffee and a chocolate chip muffin. Instead it's Mum's number flashing up. Oh crap, she's obviously calling about the ceiling cost.

'Hi, Mum.'

'Brooke.' She always states my name rather than making it sound friendly. 'I have the cost of the ceiling.'

'I'm fine thanks, Mother,' I snarl sarcastically. 'How

are you?'

She sighs down the line. 'I'm very stressed actually, Brooke. Having to sort this ceiling out has completely taken up my time.'

I roll my eyes even though she can't see me. 'Sorry, is that your time of sitting around and drinking?'

She tuts. 'I have a very busy life, thank you, Brooke. I'm looking for a job while still looking after your two sisters.'

'Mum, they're in their twenties! You're hardly still doing school runs.'

'Avery has been very traumatised about having no ceiling. We've all had to deal with her nightmares.'

Oh, boo bloody hoo. It's the *only* thing she's had to deal with her whole life. Try having a job Avery.

'Look, whatever, I don't have time for this,' I snap, quickly losing any patience I had. 'Tell me how much.'

'Fine. It's five hundred pounds.'

'Five hundred pounds! Are you fucking joking me?' I screech.

How the hell am I going to get my hands on that kind of money? I assumed it would be no more than a hundred. Surely they can patch up that sort of thing?

'No,' Mum snaps. 'I'm not the joker in this family, Brooke. You're the one that thinks it's funny to break into people's houses and crash through their ceilings.'

I roll my eyes again, feeling the stress weighing heavily on my shoulders. 'Whatever, Mum. I've gotta go.'

I hear a kerfuffle by the door and look over to see the detective having dropped papers out of his cheap briefcase all over the floor. What a bloody idiot. They totally fooled me into thinking he was credible with that swanky office.

He finally manages to scoop them up, spots me and walks over.

'Miss Archer.' He offers a clammy hand which I'm forced to take due to me being polite. Ew.

'You said you have news?' I ask impatiently with a tight smile. I've already had my patience tested with Mum. I can't last much longer before having to scream into a pillow.

'Yes.' He sits down and attempts to put the papers back into some sort of an order.

I drum my hands on the table to try to show my agitation. He's only withholding the information of my bloody dad. Kind of a big deal here!

'I've found your father,' he announces, his hands clutching onto one piece of paper.

God, just hearing those words I've been longing to hear has my stomach doing somersaults. I mean, I guessed he had, but to have it confirmed is something else entirely.

'And?' I press, forcing myself to swallow down the lump in my throat. 'Who is he?'

He places a sheet of paper in front of me. There's a picture of a man with the same black hair and blue eyes as me. Am I really looking at my dad? As I look closer, it's clear to see it's the same man from the Polaroid picture, only now with more lines. I look so like him.

'Jonathan Archer.'

I sit quietly, dazed for a moment, my thoughts incoherent.

'Archer?' I repeat in confusion. 'But that's my surname? And my mum's. How does that work?'

It said nothing in the diary about them getting married. Not that I read further than the year I was conceived.

He nods, clearly expecting this question. 'I looked into it and it seems your mum changed her name to match yours shortly after the birth.'

My temples start to throb. 'So, she gave me his name?'

Why the hell would she do that? Honour a guy who left before I was even born. A man that wanted said baby aborted. It just doesn't make sense. Surely, she was pissed as hell at the guy?

I know she said she was in love with him, but this is

blind infatuation. I mean, maybe she was obsessed with him and turned into a crazy stalker or something. Jesus, I'll have to ask her. It's weird that I can now potentially ask him.

'So, what's his story?' I ask him, tracing the picture with my finger. This man is my dad. It still feels weird after so long of not knowing.

'He's actually the mayor of Clayton, a town about forty minutes away.'

I stare at him in horror, my lower lip trembling. Because I know Clayton. I went there once. It's down the fucking road.

When I went out looking for my father, I assumed he now lived miles away. Like "other side of the country" far away from me. But forty bloody minutes away? How could he have been so close yet refused to ever get in contact with me? What the fuck?

'He's married with two sons and a daughter,' he continues. 'Been the mayor there for six years.'

He carries on talking but I can't process it. My head is now spinning. I always assumed I'd find him and he'd be shocked to see me. But how could he continue with his life knowing his son or daughter was just forty minutes away?

I could have bumped into him on the street and not even known. I can't help but feel like unwanted trash.

Like I'm not good enough for him and his sparkly new life. I'm just a mistake he wished was aborted. Not someone he's always wondered about. God, I've been so naïve.

I stand up, startling him. 'I'm sorry. I have to go.'

Then I rush out of the shop before he can open his mouth to speak. I hurry down the road, my legs forcing me into a jog. Before I know it I'm full on sprinting home.

Because I cannot break until I close that door behind me. I *cannot* cry in public.

I put the key in the lock with shaking hands and let myself in. Erica turns to me with a smile which drops off her face as soon as she takes in my features.

'Oh my God, what's happened?'

'Nothing!' I bark, running to my bedroom. I slam the door behind me and turn the lock, crumpling down to the floor.

Big fat ugly tears streak down my face, splashing onto the wooden floor beneath me. I've never felt so worthless in all my life.

Wednesday 16th August

So, I've called in sick today as I can't face people. I just can't. Right now, I don't even care if I get pulled from the project. I'd be no use to anyone.

Erica forced her way in here last night and demanded to know what was wrong. I told her the basics, but it's like any energy I've ever had has been sucked out of me. I have zero get up and go.

So today is going to be a me day. I'm not getting washed or dressed. Instead I'm going to watch a few films and eat all the food in the house. Maybe have a bit more of a cry. It's amazing how my body can produce even more tears. I could have filled a bath with them last night.

Really, I don't even know why I've got so upset. I knew my dad left before I was born and that he would have moved on with his life. But to hear he has a brand new wonderful family and is a bloody mayor. A successful family man that everyone looks up to? Children he doted on and probably read bedtime stories to. Well, it's too much to handle. A step too far. And now I'm crying again.

I don't know what I was hoping for. I suppose in a way I was hoping to find a lonely man looking for the daughter he left behind. Not someone who's so clearly moved on.

And it's not like I can run into my mum's arms to be comforted. She's hardly the maternal type. If I turned up crying, she'd probably just roll her eyes and tell me to pull myself together. Plus, she'd be pissed that I went behind her back to find him.

But I don't need her. I don't need anyone. My friends are my support and that's all I need. No, all I *choose* to let in my life. But for once I wish I had a man's arms to fall into. And not just any man's, but Nicholas'. See how weak I've become?

Banging at the front door startles me so much I spill my coffee onto my flamingo bedspread. Jesus!

I roll my eyes, dragging myself out of bed, vowing to kill the postman. Damn Erica and her bloody Amazon Prime deliveries. No wonder she's always skint.

I open the door, ready to lash out, but instead stop dead in my tracks when I see Nicholas there instead.

He's leaning against the doorframe, his navy hoodie pulled over his bowed down head. He looks up at me, his face tormented. My God, what's happened to him?

'Brooke,' he whispers, almost like a prayer.

I open my mouth to speak, but don't get a chance. He's already pushing off the wall and ensconcing me in his arms. My head hits his chest with a thump. What the hell?

I give myself a minute to collect myself and then a second longer to enjoy it, pushing my face into him, gripping onto the edge of his hoodie.

'Nicholas?' I mumble through the material. 'What

are you doing here? Has something happened?'

He strokes my hair with his hand, still not letting me move. 'I couldn't get hold of you so I rang Erica, and she told me. I'm so sorry.'

She told him? Why the hell would she do that? I don't want to look vulnerable in front of him or anyone else for that matter.

'I'm fine,' I insist, pushing him back.

There was me thinking up worst case scenarios like that Erica had been in an accident. No, she's just been shouting her mouth off instead. I wonder who else knows by now. Probably half of Brighton.

He pulls me back in immediately, ignoring my protests. 'You don't have to be strong in front of me. You can let it out.'

God, I hate hearing soppy shit like that. *Let it all out.*

But strangely enough just hearing him say those words; allowing me to break in front of him, is my undoing. I take a deep breath, the emotion rising quickly in my throat. I do not want to let go in front of him. For him to see me this emotional.

'I'm fine,' I insist, trying to pull away again. 'Nicholas, I don't know what you want from me, but I won't cry.'

He finally lets me pull away, taking me by my chin

and forcing me to look up at him. The minute I look into his midnight blue eyes it's as if they pull me under his spell. I fall into him, every wall I've ever built up comes crumbling down. A barely audible sob escapes my mouth.

He pulls me closer into him before scooping me up, taking my feet off the floor and carrying me effortlessly over to the sofa. He sits down, putting me onto his lap, pulling my hair out of my face and rubbing my back. God, it feels heavenly.

'Do you want to talk about it?'

'No.' I sniff. 'I really don't.'

'Okay,' he nods, tucking my head under his chin. His scent of grapefruit, sandalwood and musk invades my nostrils, bringing a sense of calm over me.

I sigh, the emotions fresh again. 'It's just.' I swallow down the lump in my throat. 'He's been so fucking close this whole time.'

'I know,' he nods, squeezing his arms around me tighter.

I pull away. 'You know? What do you mean, you *know*?' Did Erica tell him where he lives? Jesus, Erica, way to keep a secret!

He runs his hand through his hair making it stick up in all directions. 'I... kind of tracked him online once you'd told me you were looking for him.'

My eyes nearly jump out of their sockets. 'How the hell did you do that?'

He looks down at the floor. 'I told you, I'm good at hacking shit. I knew you'd be upset once you found out.'

I know I should be distraught that he looked into my past without my permission, but I can't help but feel treasured. He cares about me that much that he felt compelled to look him up? He's been preparing for my reaction once I found out. It's hard to be upset when someone cares that much.

'Can you believe him?' I sniff. 'Knowing you have a daughter forty minutes away and not giving a shit? What kind of man is he?'

'You're assuming he knew. Your mum put down unknown on your birth certificate. Maybe she never actually told him.'

I frown. 'My birth certificate?' He found my *birth certificate?*

'Okay, so now I look a bit stalky,' he admits on a sigh. 'But I told you, everyone has a paper trail.'

I try to ignore the fact he's gone above and beyond to find my dad and try to focus on what he's saying. No, mum told him she was going to have me. He knew I would exist.

Unless he assumed I'd come looking for him if I wanted to know him. God, the whole thing is so bloody confusing.

Quickly I wipe the tears off my cheeks. 'I don't know why I'm being so stupid, anyway. I've never even met the guy and here I am getting all wound up over him.'

He tucks some of my hair behind my ear. 'Yeah, but that doesn't stop you from imagining him being a great person and a heroic dad to you. I get it.'

Does he mean he's wondered about his mum?

'Do you often think about your mum?' I ask bravely.

He smiles sadly, his eyes distant. 'Sometimes,' he admits on a sigh. 'But it's always in a fairy tale kind of way. I know I could find her if I tried, but I refuse to go looking for someone who willingly left.'

Bless him. At least I can convince myself that my dad left before he knew me. To think that if he'd have got to know me, he would have never left in a million years. But to have your mum walk out when you're seven. That's got to hurt.

'So, do you think I'm stupid for doing this?' I can't help but ask. 'Going after him, I mean?'

'No.' He shakes his head adamantly. 'You don't know the story. I think you did the right thing.'

'Yeah, because it's brought me nothing but happiness,' I deadpan, wiping away a stray tear from my nose.

He pulls me into his chest tighter. 'When I was

younger, I used to make up stories in my head, for why my mum left. One of the stories was that she was an FBI agent who had to go into hiding or they'd threaten her family. It made me feel better.'

I look up at the wounded soul in front of me. God, no wonder he's known as being possessive and clingy. He's been through so much, not having a mother's touch. Not that mine was mother of the year, but she was still there. It's not too crazy to think that when he falls in love with someone he clings on extra tight.

'What can I do to make it better?' he asks, sweeping my hair away from my face.

Bless him. How can he always be thinking about me when my heart hurts the most when I see him so sombre?

I think about his question for a second. It's hard to concentrate when my body is weighed down by this overwhelming sadness.

'I'm just so tired. So I think I'm gonna go back to sleep.' I realise it's only 3pm, but it's as if my body is broken right now.

He nods. 'Okay. You go. I'll be here when you wake up.'

God, how can this beautiful creature be that bothered with little old me? To put me first and drop everything. My own mother's never done it.

I remember when I first started my periods, and I

called her from a local cafe. She said she'd be there straight away, but she took three hours to turn up. In the end, the waitress had taken pity on me and given me a sanitary towel. Mum was too busy with her then current boyfriend.

'Can you come sleep with me?' I ask, before considering how desperate I sound.

He smiles, so beautifully I want to jump up and sit on his face. 'Of course, I can.'

He takes my outstretched hand and lets me lead him to the bedroom where he kicks off his jacket and shoes before moving the duvet back. He pulls me into his warm chest which is quickly becoming my favourite place, wrapping me up in his arms and making me feel the most protected I ever have in my life. Would it be so bad to be possessed by this man?

Chapter 12

Thursday 17th August

I wake to find him staring at me. I almost jump out of my skin, forgetting why he's even here.

'Jesus!'

'Shit, sorry,' he laughs, showing off the most adorable smile. He looks almost boyish. 'I didn't mean to freak you out.'

I raise my eyebrows at him. 'Well, what kind of reaction did you expect when you were watching someone sleep?'

Then I remember I got caught doing exactly the same thing when I stayed at his.

He reaches out and tucks a stray bit of my hair behind my ear. 'Sorry. It's just that you look so angelic when you're asleep.'

I snort. 'So, a little different to the awake me then,' I deadpan.

'You could say that,' he smiles with knowing eyes. His eyes are so powerful as if he can see the truth in any words I speak.

'What time is it, anyway?' I ask on a stretch.

He looks at his wrist watch. 'It's 6pm.'

My eyes nearly bulge out of their sockets. 'Shit! I slept all day?'

'Yep,' he nods with a twinkle in his eyes. God, why is it every time he looks at me it's as if he can see right into my soul? It's unnerving as hell.

'I've been awake for hours. Every time I tried to go on my phone you'd stir and shout out something about pineapples.'

My eyes widen, paranoia sweeping over me. Well that's mortifying. 'Oops.'

He grins, a mischievous glint in his eyes. 'Don't worry. I still managed to get a quick video.'

'WHAT?'

He's joking, right?

He fiddles around on his phone, a second later pressing play to a video of me sleeping and he's right. Every now and again I stir and shout out 'pineapple.' How bloody random. You'd at least think I'd go for a penis shaped fruit, like a good old banana. But a pineapple? I don't even like pineapple. Maybe I need to see a psychiatrist.

'Anyway, I've been thinking,' he announces, suddenly appearing nervous. 'We should go and find your dad.'

I scoff. 'Sorry, what now?'

'Well, I've clearly had a ridiculously long amount of time to think about it while you've been dreaming of pineapples.' He pauses to smirk at me. 'And I just think you'll only keep wondering. Best to just pull the plaster off and do it now while I'm here.'

While he's here? He wants to support me with this? I don't even know if I want to see my dad. It might make me cry again.

'Shouldn't you be driving back for work?' I ask, trying to shift the attention back to him.

Surely they're pissed at him already? Not that my work will be impressed with me either.

He scoffs. 'I can work from anywhere. They're too scared to lose me to tell me otherwise. They know I'd hack the company and fuck everything up.'

I laugh, loving this cocksure version of him. 'Alright, Mr Cocky. So, you think we should just go to his house and ask him these awkward questions, do you?'

'Yep,' he nods, as if it's that straightforward. 'Why not?'

'Err... because maybe I have a little more self-respect and want to retain some dignity?'

He raises his eyebrow comically. I burst out laughing.

'Okay, fine. I'll get dressed.'

We pull up outside his house about an hour later. My father's house. It still feels weird to even think that. I look up at the detached imposing house, ivy trailing around the big, red, glossy front door.

This is how I could have grown up. In a nice house with fancy cars in the driveway. It hurts me deep inside to think instead I grew up on the mouldy council estate I did, shoved in the box room and taunted by the evil stepsisters.

'Are you ready?' he asks, his hand still on the steering wheel. God, he looks edible behind the wheel. Even if it is just a Ford Fiesta.

'No, I'm nowhere near ready,' I answer honestly. 'I don't think I ever will be, but I know I should do this.' Especially after driving an hour here. 'Will you come with me?' I blush, having no control of my cheeks.

He raises his eyebrows, his face its usual impassive stare. 'Are you sure you wouldn't rather speak to him by yourself?'

'No,' I admit, embarrassed by my own weakness. How is it I've come to rely on this guy in such a short space of time? 'I kind of feel like I need the support right now.'

He pulls out the hem of his black t-shirt, looking himself over. 'Aren't you scared the minute he sees some big tattooed bloke he'll be slamming the door and calling the police?' He grins, as if the idea entertains him.

'It is a bit of a posh neighbourhood, isn't it,' I admit looking around at a woman walking her poodle, who's staring at Nicholas. 'She's probably off to raise the alarm with the neighbourhood watch.'

He snorts out a laugh. 'Come on then. Before we get asked to leave.'

He runs around to my side of the car, taking my hand the minute I'm out. He's such an old school gentleman. God, it feels good to have someone to lean on right now. I know I could have asked Erica or one of the other girls to come with me, but he really knows what it feels like to be abandoned by a parent. Erica has no idea how that feels.

I knock on the door with my free hand, shaking like a leaf. I hope to God he answers the door and not his wife or kids. God, what am I going to say if they do? I'll have to pretend I'm a door-to-door saleswoman. How I'll explain Nicholas, I'm not sure.

Then the door opens and there in front of me stands the man from the picture. The man who fathered me.

The man that wanted me aborted.

He looks even more like me in the flesh, all black hair and identical blue eyes. His face drops as soon as he looks into my eyes.

'Brooke?'

I stand back, my jaw dropping. 'You... you know my name?' How the hell is this possible?

He walks out of the door, pulling it almost closed behind him. 'Of course, I do,' he says on a whisper. 'Does that mean you know who *I* am?'

What on earth is going on here?

'My... dad?' I ask feebly.

'Shush!' he hisses. I jump from the change in tone. 'My family are home.'

Ouch. That hurts way more than I thought it would. *His family*. I'm not part of that. Even though we share the same blood, he'll only ever consider me a stranger, a past inconvenience.

I snort, curling up my lip in distaste. 'So, I take it I'm still your dirty little secret?'

Nicholas' hand squeezes mine in support. I look down at it, so grateful he's here.

The stranger grimaces quite apologetically. 'My children aren't aware of you and I'd prefer to keep it that way. Look, I can arrange to meet you at another date and time if you'd like?'

I snort, completely unladylike. 'Don't bother,' I turn to leave, but Nicholas pulls me back.

I look back and concentrate on Nicholas' eyes. What is he trying to communicate? Why isn't he letting me leave?

'Don't do that. Ask him whatever you want.' He turns back to my dad. 'We just travelled forty-five minutes to get here. The least you can do is hear her out.' His face is murderous.

My dad looks majorly inconvenienced. He lets out a sigh, hand on his hip. 'What is it you need answering so urgently?'

Well now that I'm put on the spot here I can't think of one sensible question to ask.

'I... I...' I stammer, my tongue shaking with nerves.

'Dad?' a voice calls from inside. 'Who is it?' The door is pulled open by a guy around my age. Jesus, how quickly did he have another kid after leaving my mum high and dry?

'Nothing, son,' he says quickly. 'Just some people asking about my next mayoral election.'

'Oh,' he says with a frown, looking me over suspiciously. 'Okay.' He looks to me with curious eyes.

That's when I see it. A memory flashing through my head. No, it can't be. Can it?

I've met him before in a club in Brighton. Oh, dear

God. I made out with him. Oh my fucking god, I've made out with my brother.

My stomach lurches violently, cold sweat dripping down my spine. Vomit spills up my throat, forcing me to spew uncontrollably all over his flower beds.

Oh my God. Like this couldn't get more awful.

'What the hell are you doing?' Dad hisses, as if I'm a major inconvenience. I am just that, an inconvenience in his perfect life.

I can't look at him because I'm too busy crying, more vomit finding its way up when I think that I had my own half-brother's tongue in my mouth. Yep, here I go again.

'Leave her the fuck alone,' Nicholas snarls, pulling my hair back from my face. This is fast becoming a habit for us. 'Haven't you done enough damage?'

'I need you off my property, right now,' he demands in a harsh voice.

God, this is *so* not how I saw my first meeting with him going.

'Dad, who are these people?' the guy I now know as the brother I made out with asks.

'I said LEAVE!'

Nicholas' hands leave my hair and I hear a smacking of skin. I turn to see poor Daddio with a bloody nose. Nicholas is shaking his hand. Wait, did he just punch him?

'Nicholas! What the hell did you do?' I shriek, grabbing his wrist to inspect his pink knuckles.

A police siren sounds behind us. We turn to stare at the police car. You have *got* to be kidding me.

A policeman gets out with his colleague. 'Mayor Archer? We've been informed of suspicious characters bothering you by your neighbourhood watch? Has this man just assaulted you?'

Oh, Jesus Christ. I was right about the poodle walking bitch. She's gone and called the pigs. And of course, it doesn't look good with him having a bloody nose.

'Arrest him!' his son shouts pointing an incriminating finger at Nicholas. 'He just punched my dad.'

The policeman doesn't miss a beat. He pushes Nicholas against the wall and slaps his wrists behind him in cuffs.

'Wait, this is a misunderstanding,' I shout at the police man. 'Let him go!'

'Did he not just punch Mayor Archer?' he asks me sarcastically with a quirked eyebrow.

'I hit him,' Nicholas admits, not a hint of shame or remorse in his voice.

'Shut up, Nicholas!' I hiss. He's *really* not helping the situation.

'We'll be bringing him down the station,' the policeman explains, already carting him off towards the car. 'I suggest you follow in your car if you'd like to find out what's going to happen to him.'

For fuck's sake! I was hoping someone would step in and tell them there was no need for police involvement, but my dad just stands there with his arms crossed over his chest, watching. What an arsehole.

He's put in their police car, leaving me to rush to his car. Shit, I haven't driven a car that isn't automatic in years!

I stall the whole way there but manage to follow it to the rundown looking station. What kind of hick town is this?

I rush in telling the old man on reception who I'm here for.

'Wait here please.'

I sit down on the dirty red plastic chairs and wait thirty minutes until eventually Nicholas comes out, flexing his hands, obviously trying to bring some blood back into them after having the handcuffs on.

'Are you okay?' I ask, rushing to him, scanning my eyes over his body to find any signs of mistreatment.

'Yeah, I'm fine,' he shrugs, not seeming to enjoy my undivided attention. 'Apparently your dad didn't press charges so they couldn't hold me.'

I snort. 'That was nice of him,' I snarl sarcastically. He could have stopped this all before Nicholas was even arrested.

He smiles sadly. 'Sorry. I know tonight wasn't about me, but I just couldn't fucking stand him treating you like that.'

I sigh, resigned to the whole awful situation. 'I don't know why I expected more.'

He grimaces, taking my hand. 'I'm sorry I forced you to come.'

Does he blame himself?

'It's not your fault this happened, Nicholas.' I squeeze his hand. 'You were right for me to get it over and done with, even if it did end disastrously.'

'Maybe,' he verbally agrees, though his face doesn't match his words. 'What was with the being sick. anyway?'

Oh God, why did he have to remind me?

'You been eating more hotdogs behind my back?' His face is impassive to anyone else, but I can see the slightest curl of his lip.

I elbow him in the chest. He barely reacts.

I shudder just thinking about it, the kissing of my own brother. 'I can't even talk about it. It's too disturbing for words. I just... I can't.'

He grins, sniffing out a funny story. Funny to *him*

maybe. 'Come on. What is it?'

Oh God. Why is it I feel the need to tell this guy everything?

I gulp. 'His son.' I place my eyes on the ground, too ashamed to look at him.

'What about his son?' I keep my eyes focused on his Vans. 'No!' I look up to find him grinning, recognition in his eyes. 'Please tell me you haven't shagged him?'

I push him away childishly. 'Not that bad!'

'What then?' he asks, pushing me lightly back.

'But... oh God, I could vomit again. We did... make out in a club once.' I start retching again, turning myself away so I don't ruin his shoes.

'Hey, calm down.' He starts rubbing my back in soothing circles. 'It's fine. You didn't know.'

'That doesn't matter. It's so fucking twisted!' I shriek. 'I could have deformed future children for all I know!'

He laughs, raising his eyebrows comically. 'Why, because you swapped spit once upon a time?'

'Don't say it out loud!' I screech, pulling him away from people and towards the car. I hope to God no-one overheard me. 'The worst thing is that I was attracted to him. My own brother. I'm like one of those incestuous hillbillies that marries their cousin, except it's my fucking brother!'

He chuckles so hard he doubles over, clutching his stomach. 'Stop, you're killing me!' He straightens up when I glare at him, unimpressed. 'It's really not that bad. You didn't know.'

I wrap my arms around myself.

'Yeah, well that's not going to stop the nightmares.'

He wraps an arm around my shoulder with a snort. 'Come on Brooketini, let's go home.'

Why is it that the more time I spend with this dude the more *he* feels like home?

Chapter 13

Thursday 17th August Continued

The drive home is quiet, so peaceful that I find myself unable to keep my heavy eyelids open. Before I know it, I'm drifting off to sleep.

When I wake I find I'm being carried, Nicholas' arms under my neck and my knees. I push my face into his chest, the street lights straining my tired eyes and his calming scent settling me again.

He manages to open my front door with keys he must have taken from my bag and carries me effortlessly through to my bedroom as if I weigh no more than a feather. He yanks back the cover, depositing me on my sheets.

Now fully awake, I keep my hands around his neck as he attempts to back away. Now I've had him in my bed it's as if it feels empty and desolate without him.

'Stay,' I plead in a whisper.

Only the streetlight illuminates his features, but it's enough to see his eyes cloud over with some emotion, almost as if he's battling himself.

He eventually nods. 'I'll sleep on the sofa.'

'Please, don't,' I whimper pathetically. 'Sleep here with me.'

I reach my lips up to meet his, but he takes my hands from around his neck and pushes me away. The rejection fully awakens me. Ouch. There's only so much rejection a girl can take in one day.

'Brooke, I can't,' he whispers. 'I told you. Once we're together, there's no going back. I'll unleash full psycho and you don't want that.'

The pull towards him is undeniable. There's no strength left within me to resist. No strength to keep me from melting for him. I need him in my bed. In my life.

'For you,' I whisper back, everything suddenly so clear. 'For you, I'll try it. Unleash the psycho.'

I push my lips to his, sealing contact this time. I run my fingers through his hair, grasping a bunch of it hungrily. He pulls back again, warning me with his eyes while they're still clouded with hunger.

'I mean it Brooke. No going back.'

'I'm yours,' I practically purr. 'Fuck me,' I plead, reaching down to grab the bulge in his jeans. Fuck, he's enormous.

He sighs, his mouth quirking into a smile. 'Always so romantic.'

'Please,' I beg, shamelessly letting out a desperate groan as I press my chest against his.

'Fine, but you asked for it.'

He takes a handful of my hair, yanking it back to expose my neck. I gasp from the sudden discomfort. He smells my neck, taking an inhale as if I'm a drug, then he's licking and suckling, nipping me every so often. I wrench his hand out of my hair and pull him onto me fully.

I trace the outline of his back before grabbing the bottom of his t-shirt and yanking it up over his head. He helps me free him, his hair standing up in every direction. It makes him look sexy as sin. He grins back at me and in that instant, I've never felt happier in my life.

He pushes my vest off my shoulders and starts kissing along my collarbone. Oh God, I'll take any of his clinginess if it means I get to experience this regularly.

He kisses me again on the mouth, pushing his tongue inside to meet my own. Claiming me possessively. He tastes of something dark and compelling. I groan, needing more.

He grunts, his erection straining further against my stomach through the thin layer of denim. I have to feel him. I grab the button of his jeans and yank until it falls open. My finger catches his fly and drags it all the way down. His erection springs free, falling into my palm. My God, he's a big boy.

I tuck my thumbs into the side of his boxer shorts and attempt to drag them down. He helps me by lifting his hips and dragging down one side until he's completely naked, his bare arse in my other palm.

God, just feeling the velvety skin of his dick in my hand does wild things to me.

He takes hold of my neck with one hand palming my breast through my bra with the other. Next he takes the hem of my vest top, yanking it off over my head. It gives me a second to smile meekly back up to him.

'Are you okay?' he asks, nothing but concerned sincerity in his eyes.

I blink up at him, suddenly feeling on the verge of tears. What the hell is wrong with me? I want this.

'Sorry,' I sniff, my eyes filling with tears. 'I don't know why I'm suddenly upset.'

He immediately stops and wraps me in his arms, laying on the bed and pulling me into him. I let the tears drip onto his chest. Why the hell am I crying? I must be due on.

'Sshh,' he insists, rocking me like a baby. 'You've had a rough night. You met your dad for the first time and realised you made out with your brother.' I can tell just from the muscles in his neck that he's smiling.

'Don't!' I chuckle, wiping the tears with the back of my hand. 'It's not funny.'

He rolls me over so he's above me again, tucking some of my hair behind my ear. I'm starting to realise he does it as a sign of affection.

'Look, now you're mine, my first priority is to look after you. Right now, you've been through a lot and I think you need your sleep.'

I feel so bad. Talk about a blue balls tease. I was desperate for it a minute ago. I reach for his cock again.

'Let me at least give you a hand job.'

His mouth falls open. He takes my hand from him, pulling his boxer shorts back up.

'No, Brooke. Sleep. Now.'

I sigh, hugging him tighter. 'You're no fun.'

Friday 18th August

I wake up to him bringing me tea and toast dressed in just his boxers. Fuck me, he looks hot! All slim, toned torso and those beautiful athletic footballer legs completely covered in tattoos. I can't help but let a stupid grin spread onto my face.

'Morning,' he says with a sly grin.

God, how can he be so delicious? Seeing him like this, half naked, in my bedroom and carrying me food; God, it just makes me want to make him a permanent feature.

'Thought you'd need some food. You know, after the shock yesterday.'

I sit up, pushing my hair out of my face. 'Thank you.'

I snag a slice of toast as soon as he places them down onto my bedside table. Mmm, even his toast is perfect.

He sits down on the edge of the bed. I wish he'd pull the cover back and get in.

'So, are you coming back to bed?' I ask as seductively as I can.

He scrubs his face with his hands. 'I wish I could, but I should really get back.'

'Oh.' I can't hide the disappointment in my voice.

Could he have just enjoyed the whole chase and now that he's claimed me he's off?

He tips my chin up to look at him, depositing a soft kiss on my lips. 'Don't be worried. You have me. But I promised my dad I'd help him with something.'

I smile, feeling better immediately. 'Okay.'

I'm desperate to ask when I'll see him again, but I must try to play it cool.

He gets dressed while I munch on my toast and

drink my tea. Then he gives me one final belly bursting kiss, and he's gone. I don't care what he says. I'm feeling vulnerable. And this is why I fucking hate relationships.

I quickly get dressed and head straight to visit Nan. I don't want Erica to catch me and quiz me about what's going on between me and Nicholas.

As soon as I open her room, the familiar smell of talcum powder and lavender greets me. I already feel calmer.

Nan's sat at her small table and chairs, reading a newspaper.

She lowers her reading glasses. 'Hello, sweetheart. I wasn't expecting you today.'

I throw myself down on her bed. 'Surprise! I need chocolate.'

She chuckles, getting out her stash from her bedside table. I open a packet of Malteasers.

'So...' she pries, raising her eyebrows and dropping her chin. 'Why the chocolate? What's the drama?'

Dammit, she knows me too well.

'Ugh, why are men so bloody complicated?' I stuff a handful of Malteasers into my mouth to stop myself from elaborating. I don't want Nan to know about Nicholas yet. Wanting to keep him my little secret for now.

She smiles knowingly. 'That's just the way they are sometimes. The good thing about being a strong woman is that we don't *need* men. They're lucky if we *want* them.'

I sigh. God, I love this woman.

'I love your outlook on life.' She never fails to make me feel better.

'That's what I'm here for, sweetheart. Now what do you say we put on Dirty Dancing and stuff our faces with more rubbish? I have a chocolate orange around here somewhere.'

I could cry with happiness. Yep, definitely due on the old period. God, I love this woman.

Chapter 14

Tuesday 22nd August

It's been four days. Four days and I still haven't heard from him since he kissed me goodbye that morning. It's killing me. Literally killing me.

Of course, I've thought about calling or texting him loads of times, but why the hell should I? He's the one that gave me the whole *"I'm an obsessive guy"* speech and then he just fucks off without a thought. Especially when he knows I'm still reeling from finding out about my dad.

I mean, I could be fucking another guy for all he knows. Where's the psycho I was promised?

That's it. I've decided. I'm going out. Not sit inside like some fucking nineteen-fifties housewife waiting for her man to call. No, I'm gonna call the girls and we're gonna tear up Brighton.

Within a couple of hours, after a little persuasion,

we're in Phoenix dancing to some banging hits. It helped that Alice has just been asked to showcase her photography in an exhibition in a few weeks. She's celebrating while I'm commiserating.

I don't know why but just moving my hips to the beat gets me horny as hell.

After talking it out with the girls I've decided that Nicholas is a fuck boy, just like Tom. The girls have actually said the opposite, but I'm so irrationally angry every time I think of him ignoring me.

How dare he deprive me of this. Dangle the carrot and then take it away. Dangle the dick more like. It must be because I chickened out on the sex and ended up blubbing all over him like a nutcase. Who can blame him really?

I get my phone out and decide right there and then that I'm taking control again. How dare he ignore me.

Well, you talk a lot of shit, don't you?! All, once you're mine there's no going back. Well I want to go back. Back to when you gave a shit!

I decide to type another straight after. First, I take another gulp of my drink.

I don't know why I fucking bothered with you. You're just a fuck boy like Tom. And to think you tried to make out you were better than him. That's the worst kind of fuck boy.

I'm feeling better the more I type out what I'm feeling. It's therapeutic.

I don't even know why I'm bothered. You're not all that.

I look around the club, trying to find one of the girls. Instead I find that same guy watching me again. Okay, this is getting weird. He's definitely following me. I go to confront him when a text pings through. I nearly drop the phone with excitement. Is it him? My heart sinks when I see it's my occasional fuck Simon. I glance back at the crowd but he's gone. Dammit. I open the text from Simon instead.

Hey good looking. Staying at hotel Grandon tonight if you fancy keeping me company? x

I think about it for a second. Why the fuck not? Simon's a great fuck, and it's not like that wank stain Nicholas is beating down my door. Probably shagging another bird in Peterborough, laughing over my abusive texts. Prick.

'Who are you texting?' Alice asks, snatching my phone off me.

'I was telling Nicholas to go fuck himself,' I admit proudly, hand on my hip.

Her jaw drops. 'Jesus, Brooke! I've never seen you hung up on a man like this before. Right, I'm confiscating this phone so you don't do something you'll regret.'

I scoff. 'Whatever, I don't need it, anyway. I'm going to get another drink.'

I turn and walk away from her, but instead of heading to the bar I head for the door.

Ignoring the check-in desk, I go straight to the elevator. Simon only ever checks into the same room. Sometimes I wonder how he always seems to get it at such short notice, but I know he's here a lot with work. Plus, I don't really care enough to ask. You see, Simon is fit. No, scratch that, he's fit as fuck. All blonde hair and dark olive eyes. And right now, I need someone to distract me.

I knock on the door, adjusting my boobs in my dress. God, it seems I'm a lot more drunk than I thought. I hope my face doesn't look a mess.

He swings the door open before I have a chance to check, already in just a towel, still wet from a shower, exposing his perfectly bronzed six-pack. I can't help but compare it to Nicholas' fully tattooed one.

'Brooke,' he practically purrs, undressing me with his eyes.

It feels good for someone to want me. I push him backwards into the room, kissing him aggressively.

Tonight, I just want raw, dirty sex. I know Simon can give me that.

I shove him onto the edge of the bed, untie the towel and let his already erect dick spring free. My God, it's beautiful. Not as beautiful as Nicholas' but it's still pretty great.

I smile, biting my lip seductively. His eyes blaze with lust. I lower my lips around his cock, sliding him into my mouth. I suck with a vengeance, swirling my tongue over the tip of his head every now and again making him flinch and fist my hair in his hand.

This is what I need. To feel powerful and in control. Not at a man's mercy.

The door suddenly bangs. I stop and look up at him. 'Are you expecting anybody?'

I hope to God he's not thinking I'll be into a threesome. I am not into women. If I was I'd just marry Molly and I only drunkenly suggested we kiss once. Okay, it was twice but everyone gets needy on New Year's Eve, right?

'Probably just room service or something.' He stands up with a huff, begrudgingly wrapping the towel around him.

He opens the door. 'No thank—' He stops mid-sentence. I watch as his back muscles tense.

Who the hell is it?

I look around, wondering why he's suddenly so quiet. A blonde-haired woman with perfectly blow dried short hair is staring at him. Who the hell is this?

'You absolute bastard!' she shouts, hitting him in the chest.

Whoa, who the fuck is this nutcase?

'I knew it! I fucking knew it!' she screams, between sobs.

Why the hell isn't he doing anything? Demanding she leaves the room? Telling her she's got the wrong person. Maybe I should call security.

'Who the fuck is this?' I ask, standing up, hand on my hip.

She turns to glare at me, her eyes fired with hatred. 'More like who the fuck are *you!* As for me, I'm his wife!'

His wife? His fucking *wife?* The room starts spinning around me, the tequila shots making themselves known. He's married? Bloody *married?*

I suppose that would make sense if I ever stopped to think about it. He, like me, has never wanted more and we've only ever met here or at mine whenever he's in town.

'You're married?' I can't help but ask, just to clarify.

He bows his head. 'Yes.'

'Fuck. You bastard.' I punch him in the back, it being an instant stupid reaction. I should have at least gone for his face. Instead I end up injuring my own hand. I knew I should have taken Alice's advice about how to punch correctly.

'Don't you dare hit my husband!' she screams at me, her neck red and blotchy.

I scoff. 'Are you fucking joking, love? The guy's been fucking me for months! Hardly the time to stand up for the pig.'

She takes a large, harsh intake of breath. 'You're just a little whore.' She launches herself at me, pushing me back onto the bed. Then she's slapping me round the face frantically.

I try to protect myself by shielding my face with my arms and edge away. I fall off the other side of the bed and in doing so hit my cheek on the edge of the bedside table. Shit, that hurts like a motherfucker!

I look up to see Simon holding her back, her face enraged. 'Get out of here while you can,' he shouts at me.

I can't believe the fucking cheek of him! Shouting for *me* to leave. I'm not the two-timing husband. Well fuck this. I grab my purse and hightail it out of there.

Just when you think your night couldn't get any worse.

I make my way home by foot. Without my phone, I

can't get an Uber and truth be told, I need the fresh air to think. God, if my Nan knew I was walking alone at this time of night she'd go spare. Lucky for me she's tucked up in her care home. I suppose I should be being more careful now that I'm pretty sure I have a stalker, but in the mood I'm currently in, I dare some bastard to try to attack me. It'd give me the excuse I need to let out this rage.

I finally make it to the flat, my feet tired and my body craving the rest that only a shower and my bed can provide. I can hear talking as I unlock the door, my limbs heavy. Oh God, I hope they haven't brought people back. I could do without a party right now. Christ, I really am getting old.

I walk into the kitchen to find all the girls in there talking with Jack. Some are sitting on the worktop, the others at the kitchen table.

'She's here! Thank God,' Erica says to someone down the phone.

'Where the fuck have you been?' Evelyn shouts, jumping up from her chair. 'We've been worried sick, Brooke!'

I sigh, so not in the mood for this shit. Especially from Evelyn.

'Sorry, *Mum,* but last I checked I was a twenty-seven-year-old woman. Not a fucking child.'

'That's not the point, Brooke,' Alice snaps. 'You told me you were going to the bar. I was worried you were abducted or something!'

I scoff. 'Don't be so bloody dramatic.' I can't help but be bitchy. I just want to be left alone right now.

'What happened to her face? Were you mugged?' I turn my head away from her so she can't touch it.

'No. I just... fell down, is all. There's no need for you all to assume I was dead in an alley somewhere.'

'We only care,' Molly says, pulling me into a hug. Bless her. My heart melts, hugging her back. God knows I need it. 'Besides, we've needed to get hold of you.'

I pull back and look into her concerned face as she nibbles her lower lip. 'Why?'

I notice that Erica is still on the phone. She hands it over to Jack and walks over, her forehead in so deep a frown there are indents there I'm sure will last forever.

She swallows, taking my hands. 'Brooke, it's Nicholas. He's been trying to get hold of you half the night.'

Oh shit. My stomach lurches with apprehension. What's happened?

'That's him on the phone.'

I don't pause to think, I'm already grabbing the phone off Jack.

'Nicholas?'

There's a long space of silence and then 'Hi.' He sounds tired, almost defeated. 'Where have you been?'

'I think I should be asking you that, don't you?' Oh God, way to sound like a possessive nutcase of a bunny boiler, Brooke.

'Were you still at the club?'

No, I was trying to fuck a man. A married man. God, I am the worst.

'Yes, I wandered off to another club. I thought... well, I thought that you'd...' I look around, suddenly conscious of the others listening in. I walk into my room, shutting the door behind me. 'Tell me what's happened.'

'Brooke,' he sighs. 'My dad had a heart attack.'

Oh shit. Just like that my stomach falls out of my knickers. He's needed me. Needed my support and what have I been doing? Running off, having a tantrum and trying to get my knickers wet. I'm such a whore. I don't deserve him.

'Oh my God, is he okay?' I ask, more like a demand.

'Yeah. He's still in hospital, but he gave us a scare for a while. If I wouldn't have gone back that day he would have been alone. He would have died.'

'Shit.' Wait, does he blame himself? 'Do you want me to come up?'

'No, you're better off there. I just wanted to let you know. Anyway, I read your texts.'

I bow my head in shame as if he can see me.

'I'm so sorry, but I had no idea. I just thought...'

'It's pretty clear what you thought,' he interrupts. 'When are you going to realise you need to trust me?'

God, why did I have no faith in him?

'I'm so sorry.'

For everything. For so much, he has no idea.

He sighs heavily down the phone. 'It's fine.'

'I... I really feel like I should be with you.' I want to say something more profound, something with more feeling. Something that will tell him how much I feel for him, but I'm useless at this. 'Are you sure you don't want me to drive up?'

'No, it's fine.' I imagine him shaking his head. 'Just...'

'Just what? Anything?' I plead, desperate to remove some of his pain. Desperate to eradicate some of my own guilt.

'Brooke, please don't go running off on your own anymore. I worry about you.'

That's all he's worried about? Not that I'm some insecure little slut that's going to run off for another man's approval the minute I'm not getting attention.

'I won't,' I whisper, my throat closing in on me.

I might have only been in a relationship for four days but I've already won *Worst Girlfriend ever*. In the words of Cher, *If I could turn back time.*

Chapter 15

Wednesday 23rd August

I feel so helpless knowing Nicholas is having to deal with this on his own. I texted him this morning asking if he needed anything, to which he politely declined. It's all such awkward timing. We're not at a real place in our relationship yet and I had to go and confuse things further by sucking Simon's dick.

It's only just bloody started and now I'm supposed to know how to act. When the truth is that I have no idea what to do. Should I tell him? Or is it kinder for him not to know?

Work has distracted me today. At least it's taken my mind off it.

I think I've come to the conclusion that I'm going to drive up this weekend. I need to wrap my arms around him, need to see for myself how he's doing. Jack's going anyway to celebrate his birthday with the rest of the boys, and then Esme, so I can just jump in with him.

'What a day,' Steven, one of the other designers who works here says, stretching back in his chair.

'Tell me about it.' I kick my shoes off and stretch out my aching back.

'Fancy a quick bunk up before we leave?' He smiles with a cheeky wink.

Me and Steven have a shag every now and again. Nothing serious, just sex. It's mutually beneficial.

I roll my eyes. 'Afraid not. I'm actually seeing someone.'

'No way,' he says, eyes wide, mouth parted.

Alright. It's not *that* unbelievable.

'Yep. So, this,' I motion between us, 'has obviously got to stop.'

Not that it happens too often. Normally around once a month.

He nods in understanding. 'Obviously. I'm gonna miss it though.' He sits on the edge of my desk, in the process knocking over my banana milkshake. It spills all over my skirt. 'Shit, sorry!'

'Steven! For fuck's sake.' It's funny that the minute I'm not fucking him I've started to realise how bloody annoying he is.

I stand up, gritting my teeth so as not to call him every bad name under the sun. 'Right, I'm going to get this cleaned up.'

I head for the toilet, wondering if my week can get any worse.

Nicholas

I call her, needing to hear her voice. It's crazy how just the sound of it can calm my frayed nerves and right now I need it. Hearing my dad needs a stent put into his main artery has me craving her so much I physically itch.

'Hello?' a male voice answers at the other end.

My body stiffens. 'Who's this?' I bark out accusingly.

'This is Steven. Are you looking for Brooke?'

That's why I rang her phone dickhead.

'My girlfriend,' I clarify. 'Yeah.'

'She's just cleaning herself up in the bathroom. Do you want me to get her to call you back?'

The ground falls away from me. Cleaning herself up. She's fucked him. Of course she has. I'm not there and she's got needs. I should have never assumed she could handle a relationship. She said herself she was shit at them. I shouldn't have pushed her into it. But she promised. Agreed that she'd be mine. She lied to my face.

I hang up the phone, letting it smash to the ground.

It's over before it had even started. And now I have no-one.

Friday 25th August

Steven said Nicholas had called me Wednesday night. I tried to call him back but there was no answer and I haven't been able to get hold of him since. It's weird. I hope his dad is okay.

I questioned Jack this morning, but he said he hadn't heard from him either. He did however give me Charlie's number. I laughed it off at first, surely I wouldn't be desperate enough to need to call him. Turns out I was wrong. It's only 10am and I'm putting his number into my phone while in the work toilets.

'Hello?' Charlie asks tentatively.

'Charlie? It's Brooke.'

'Oh.' Is it me or did his voice just fall flat? 'Hi.'

'Hi. I'm trying to get hold of Nicholas. Apparently, he called me last night but I can't seem to get hold of him and I'm freaking out a little as I know his dad's still in hospital.'

He sighs heavily down the phone. 'Nicholas really doesn't need this right now, Brooke.'

Huh? What the hell is he talking about?

'Doesn't need *what* right now?' Is he high?

'He doesn't need some girl messing with his head, playing games with his heart. He's a sensitive guy, and he doesn't deserve to be treated like this.'

'Like what?' I shout back, enraged. What the hell am I being accused of here? 'Charlie, I have no idea what you're talking about. Last thing I knew we were good. What the hell am I supposed to have done?'

He sighs heavily again. 'He spoke to your boss last night. Found out you'd just fucked him.'

It's as if the floor falls away from me. My boss. She wasn't in yesterday. Wait, is he talking about Steven? He thinks I fucked Steven?

'Look, Brooke, if you've only been pursuing Nicholas to make Tom jealous then just stop right now. It's not fair.'

He thinks I'm really after Tom? Jesus, Charlie really thinks I'm some kind of heartless slag.

'Sorry!' I interrupt, not sounding apologetic at all. 'He thinks I slept with Steven? Why the fuck would he think that?'

He hesitates. 'Look, I don't know the full story, but that's what he told me.'

God, he's a seriously paranoid guy if he thinks that. I mean, yeah, he knows I enjoy sex, but is it too much to ask that he trusts me now we're supposedly together? He doesn't know I've already done the dirty with Simon.

'Yeah, well he's fucking wrong,' I bark, barely able to keep my anger under control. 'So bloody wrong. I need to speak to him. Where is he?' I demand, tapping my foot impatiently.

'Babe, your guess is as good as mine. I can't get a hold of him today and he's not at the hospital or at home.'

'Shit.' Immediately I know that I have to go see him. 'I'm coming down.'

'You mean you're coming up,' he says with a hint of amusement in his voice.

Is he *serious?*

'What the fuck ever, Charlie! I don't have time for a geography lesson right now.'

'Sorry,' he says, sounding sheepish.

'If you see him in the meantime, tell him I'm on my way to kick his fucking arse.'

I told work I had intense period pains and managed to grab Jack before he drove up for the weekend to visit Esme. It didn't make sense for us both to do the same journey although I'm hoping Nicholas realises what an idiot he's been and grovels to me so I can crash at his.

Not that I really deserve the grovelling after my encounter with Simon. The crazy thing is that he's going mental thinking I did this with Steven, when I did something not so dissimilar with Simon just the night before. I'm a total hypocrite, but I hate being accused of something I've not done. Besides, I thought he was fucking me around before.

If anything, how he's reacted has proved I can never tell him. The worst thing is that he's not even confronted me about this, just gone off on one. If I wasn't so obsessed with him myself, I could have gone a week without realising he was even pissed off.

Three hours later we're finally pulling into Nicholas' drive. I notice Jack sigh in relief. To say I've been bad company is an understatement. I'm lost in my own head and his incessant questions annoyed the fuck out of me.

I don't even know what Nicholas means to me, let alone trying to explain it to him. The boys seem to be so protective of him and it pisses me off. Why isn't Jack protective of me? I'm Erica's best friend. But that's the problem when you put out a bad bitch vibe, people assume you don't have feelings. That you're heartless. Well I'm not and I resent it.

The lights are off in the house with only his dad's van in the drive.

'He must already be out,' Jack says peering over the house.

'Yes, thank you, Columbo, for stating the obvious.' I

can't help but be cruel. Ugh, I should be grateful that he's driven me down here, but until I speak to Nicholas I'm going to be like a bear with a sore head.

I still get out and knock frantically at the front door. So frantically that a neighbour opens her window.

'He's not in, love,' she shouts, looking at me as if I'm majorly inconveniencing her. 'Went out a few hours ago with his big friend.'

I look to Jack who's now got out of the car. We grin at each other with amused eyes. Big friend.

'What, a chubby guy?' I ask, us both knowing full well she's talking about Charlie.

I start planning Charlie's murder for not calling me immediately. He knows how worried I am.

'No,' the neighbour says with a head shake, her curlers almost falling out. 'Big as in broad. Big strapping fellow.'

Shit. Does she mean Tom? Where the hell would they have gone? At least I don't have to murder Charlie. But with Tom anything's possible.

'Any idea where they went?' I ask, trying to communicate with my eyes how desperate I am for any information.

She grimaces. 'Well, Nicholas was holding a bottle of whiskey, so if I had to guess I'd say he's gone into town on a bender.'

Shit, shit, shit.

Upset, emotional and drunk is never a good combination.

I get my phone out and call Charlie.

'I've found him,' he answers straight away without a hello.

'Where is he?' I demand, hand on my hip.

There's a lot of background noise. 'He's in a bar called Breakaway. But... well, he's not in a good way.'

'What do you mean? Is he okay?' I press, frantically coming up with worst case scenarios.

He sighs. 'He's pretty fucking wasted. I don't think you should come up here. Why don't you hang around there and I'll bring him back soon?'

Why on earth wouldn't he want me to go to them? Unless... what is Nicholas doing that I wouldn't want to see in person? My stomach recoils. With Tom as his chaperone he could be up to all manner of things.

'What the fuck are you trying to hide, Charlie?' I practically growl.

'Nothing,' he answers quickly. Too quickly. I hear him gulp. Bloody chicken shit.

'Good, well then there's no reason why I can't come. Be there soon.'

I hang up and turn to Jack. 'He's at a bar called Breakaway?'

Jack runs his hand through his hair, avoiding eye contact. 'Brooke, are you sure this is a good idea? I mean, you don't exactly know how you're going to find him.'

I glare at him. What are they trying to hide from me?

'You either drive me yourself or I get an Uber.'

He sighs, rolling his eyes. 'Look, I'll take you, but first I have to go home to have a shower.'

'A shower?' I shriek. He's hardly dirty. 'Can't you see when there's an emergency?'

He looks down his nose at me. 'This isn't an emergency, Brooke. This is you having a bitch fit. I need to shower because this is supposed to be my weekend with my mates. Remember?'

God, I really am a shit friend.

'Sorry,' I grimace. 'Okay, I suppose I can wait.' It might give me a chance to calm down too.

We drive back to his house and he leaves me in the sitting room while he goes upstairs to shower. I apply some more lipstick in the mirror. I want to look as hot as fuck when I shout him down for accusing me of doing something I haven't. No, not even accusing me. He didn't even give me the chance to be accused, oh no, he just bloody assumed. Arsehole.

Not that I don't feel guilty about what happened

with Simon, but I feel like we were at a different stage of our relationship then.

I look as good as I can considering I've been stuck in a car for the last couple of hours.

While I wait for Jack to get ready, I settle myself down in front of the TV and turn on *A Place in the Sun.* I need something to take my mind off this whole shit show that is currently my life.

The door opens behind me. *Finally.* I don't let my eyes leave the TV, imagining myself retiring somewhere hot.

'Who the hell are you?' a voice shouts from behind me.

I turn in the chair to find a middle-aged man in just his Y fronts, his overly furry chest hair is so thick some of it is matted. I can't help but stare at it. He's staring at me with wide eyes.

'Agh!' I scream, jumping out of the seat and grabbing a weapon.

There's only a dirty coffee mug, but I still hold it out to him in warning. I don't quite know what that warning is; that I'll caffeine him to death? I pull my best ninja face. For all he knows I could be a master of Ju-Jitsu.

'Well?' He shouts, attempting to cover himself in vain. 'Who the hell are you?'

'I'm Brooke. Who the hell are you?' I shout back,

holding the coffee mug over my head.

He flinches, backing away from me. 'I'm Daniel. Jack's father. I bloody well live here. Now can I ask why *you're* here?'

His dad. Okay that makes more sense than he's a random homeless man that's broken in to rape me. He must be joking though? How can Jack have never mentioned to his dad that he lives with a Brooke? I can't help but be offended. I mean, surely he'd have at least bitched about me once. But nothing. No reaction. It stings.

'I'm here with Jack.'

Jack comes bounding down the stairs, no doubt having heard the commotion. He walks in wearing just a towel, his hair still damp. Ew, could the people around here put some damn clothes on!

'Dad, what's going on?'

His dad's eyes tighten, his nostrils flaring. 'I could ask you the same thing, boy! Who the hell is this hussy? I thought you were serious about Erica.'

Huh? I look between them both in confusion. Wait, he thinks Jack is sneaking around on Erica?

'No, Dad,' he says shaking his head. 'It's not like that. This is Brooke, my flatmate and Erica's best friend.'

He looks me up and down. 'Is this true?' he asks me,

looking over my outfit as if I'm trash. They clearly don't know fashion up here.

'Of course, it is,' I answer. 'Jesus, Jack's not my type, anyway.'

Jack scoffs, as if my answer is ridiculous. 'I'm *everyone's* type,' he says under his breath with an amused grin. He shakes his head as if attempting to pull himself together. 'Anyway, Dad, can you please put some bloody clothes on.'

He looks down at himself as if just remembering. He covers his nipples with his hands. 'Yes, of course.' He looks back at me with an uncomfortable smile. 'Lovely to meet you.'

Well, let's hope they never get married. I don't want to have to look that guy in the eye ever again.

We're finally parked up and walking towards the bar where I'll find Nicholas. In what state, I don't know. My mouth is dry, my muscles quivering in anticipation. My gut tells me I'm about to find him in a bad way.

'I'm sorry again about my dad,' Jack offers with a cringe.

I feel bad for the guy. If the situation were reversed I'd be dying of humiliation right now.

'It's fine,' I shrug. 'And look, I'm sorry I've ruined

this weekend for you. It's just that... well, Nicholas...' I sigh heavily, 'he drives me crazy.'

He smiles knowingly. 'I get it. That's how I feel about Erica.'

I stare back at him, my eyebrows squished together. Wait, Erica drives him crazy?

'Huh? You and Erica are having problems?' I ask, still in a state of shock.

He rolls his eyes. 'No, dummy. I mean she drives me crazy in a good way.'

Wait, is he trying to say I'm in love with Nicholas or something? I'm not. *Obviously,* I'm not. I've just started dating the bloody guy. I don't know how I feel about him.

But I know the thought of him hurt has me wanting to swap bodies with him, desperate to take over some of the pain he's experiencing.

Jack is a good guy. I suppose because we live together I spend most of my time being annoyed by him leaving towels on the floor, but he's good for Erica.

'Hey Jack, did Erica ever tell you about what Amber said to her?'

He frowns. 'No. Why? What did she say?'

I roll my eyes. 'I knew she wouldn't. She told her that she was a phase for you and that you were going to come running back to Peterborough soon enough.'

'You're joking?' His gaze is murderous. Wait until I tell him the rest.

'Nope. And she said she didn't want Esme seeing her again. Not until you were married.'

'No fucking way.' His fists clench against the steering wheel. 'That bitch. I knew Erica was acting strange on the way home.'

I spot the bar signage and brace myself. Whatever I feel for Nicholas, it's about to get real.

I jump out of the car, not waiting for Jack to park, and storm straight towards the bar, the loud RnB nearly bursting my eardrums.

I scan for him, but can't see any of them. Finally I spot Charlie pacing around towards the back, phone to his ear. Why does he look so jumpy? What the hell is going on?

'Charlie.' He almost drops his phone he jumps so high.

His eyes widen before rapidly blinking. 'Brooke. I told you not to come down here.' He looks behind him, his forehead furrowed.

I turn to follow his eye line. Nicholas is sitting in a booth in the corner with Tom and two girls. One of the girls is on his lap, laughing, her fake tits bouncing in his face as she strokes her fingers through his hair. *My* hair.

What. The. Actual. Fuck.

The rage burns through my veins, so strongly it feels like it's going to come bursting out of my lungs and onto the floor. Oh no, he didn't fucking think this was okay.

I race over there, grab the bitch by her hair and yank her off him. She falls back with a thud.

'Aagh!' she screams, clutching her head. 'What the fuck?'

I don't have time for this basic bitch right now. I'm too busy glaring at Nicholas. On closer inspection, it's clear to see that he's paralytic. His eyes are glassy, his head lolling around from side to side. She was basically taking advantage of him. Totally rapey.

'What the fuck, Nicholas?' I yell in his face, pushing against his chest in an attempt to sober him up.

'Brooke,' he manages, eyes narrowed as if he's trying to focus on me.

I turn to Tom, wanting to hurt someone. 'Fuck you, Tom! Is this your way of punishing me for not wanting you? To get him shit-faced and get him to fuck some random?'

'Hey!' basic bitch shouts behind me.

'I don't have time for you, bitch,' I snap, warning her with my eyes that I'm capable of just about anything right now. I turn back to Tom.

'Hey, Brooke,' Tom says, his hands up in surrender. 'He was going out regardless of me. I only came with him to make sure he was okay.'

'And what part of allowing a skank on his lap was making sure he was okay?' I snarl, my lip curling in anger.

'I'm not the one who fucked my boss!' Tom shouts back at me.

'Neither am I, dickhead!' I scream. Then I turn to Nicholas. 'I can't believe you thought that of me.'

Now that I'm looking into his tortured face my anger is replaced by betrayal. How could he think that of me? He's the one person who is supposed to believe in me, yet he threw me under the bus immediately.

Nicholas runs his hand through his hair, incapable of saying anything it seems.

'Well fuck you, Nicholas.' I feel my eyes mist up. God, I never cry in public. I need to get out of here. 'Fuck all of you. You can go to hell.'

Chapter 16

Nicholas

Monday 28th August

I can't believe I fucked up so badly. Thought so badly of her without a bit of actual evidence. But I believe her. I know she wouldn't have driven all the way up here just to scream at me if she had shagged that wanker of a boss. I still don't understand why he made out he had shagged her. Oh wait, yes, I do. Because he wants her all to himself. Just how I had her before I fucked everything up.

Now that I've sobered up I realise what a royal prick I've been. But now she won't take my calls.

'Chill out, man,' Tom says, slapping me on the back. 'Leave it until she's cooled down.'

'Really? You think she'll cool down?' I ask hopefully.

He sneers. 'Mate, I've never seen a chick so mad in my life. I have no fucking idea. I normally fuck off before they start menstruating all around me.'

I roll my eyes, clenching my fists. 'That's because you're a dick.'

The thing with me is that I'm supposed to be the good guy. I promised her the fucking world and then accused her of cheating, all within two weeks. What a twat I am.

'I should go to see her as soon as I get Dad settled back home,' I muse out loud. He's having his stent put in today. 'Explain in person.'

'I dunno,' Charlie counters, biting his lip. 'Is Brooke the kind of girl to chase? What if you scare her away?'

I think about how apprehensive she was to even embark on a proper relationship.

'That's a risk I'm gonna have to take.'

Brooke

Tuesday 29th August

I got the train back on Friday, crying all the way home. I got some funny looks, but I honestly couldn't have cared less. Who knew I even had that many tears in my body? When they say your body is eighty percent water, I must have got rid of seventy percent of that last night. By the time I got home I fell into bed, never wanting to resurface.

The worst thing about it all is that he was right in a way. I did meet up with Simon before all of this went down. I am the slut he thinks I am. And now that I've gone mad, it means I'll never be able to confess it to him.

I've fucked up any chance of ever having a healthy relationship with him. Maybe with anybody. I was right. Seems I don't deserve a normal relationship.

I'm still so downhearted. I never knew people could feel this bereaved over a guy. Now I feel terrible for all the times one of the girls has cried over a bad relationship and I've secretly laughed. Turns out I'm much more of a mess. This is just another example of how I'm not cut out for this serious relationship shit.

I finish up work and leave, noticing someone in the corner of my eye. Oh God, not the stalker again. I look over but I'm stunned to see instead it's Nicholas lurking in a corner, staring at me.

I blink my eyes and look again in case I'm dreaming. What the fuck is he doing here? Most people would take someone dodging your calls as a clear sign that the relationship is over.

What the fuck gives him the right to follow me around? Lurking in the shadows like that other weirdo?

He's the one that ruined things between us, yet he still thinks he can follow me around, controlling everything I do? I don't think so.

I storm over to him, rage burning in my veins.

'What the fuck are you doing here?' I demand.

His face is tortured, a pained stare in his blue eyes. He rocks on his heels, his hands in his pockets.

'I wanted to see you. You won't pick up your phone.'

'Yeah, it's called ignoring you.' I know it's harsh, but this is the best thing to do. We're clearly not right for each other and attempting this again would be too painful for both of us. 'That doesn't mean you should drive all the way here in the hope that I'll give you the time of day.'

He hunches his shoulders, looking at me with wide puppy dog eyes. It takes everything in me not to jump into his arms.

'I had to try. Brooke, I'm so sorry.'

The only way I'm going to get rid of him is to hurt him. Really hurt him. It might be horrible now, but it's better than us getting back together and him finding out later on about Simon. That could potentially break him for good.

'You know what?' I snap, my eyes cold, 'I really wish I'd taken Kerrie's advice.'

His eyes widen before scrunching almost shut. 'You don't mean that.'

I close my eyes, attempting to pull myself together. I cannot show any hint of emotion or he'll know my plan.

'Yes, actually, I do. She told me you were a psycho, and I never listened. But she was right. You're the nutcase she always said you were.'

His face breaks, his jaw falling open, his eyes helpless. God, I've gone too far. I've broken him. But I shouldn't care. He broke me when he had that slut on his lap right in front of me.

This is for the best, for both of us. So why do I feel so bad?

I rush towards home, only stopping when I get a text message. I take out my phone, wondering if it's him. No such luck. It's Mum.

I need that money, Brooke. Five hundred pounds. Now.

Ugh, just what I bloody need right now. How on earth am I expected to find that sort of money so quickly?

Everything together just makes me want to hurt someone. The only person I can think that deserves to get hurt is my so-called father. So, before I knew what I was doing I'd Googled our local newspaper's number and pressed dial.

'How can I help you?'

I swallow. I'm really doing this. 'Err... hi. I think I have a story for you.'

'I'll put you through.' A few beeps sound out before it clicks with an answer. 'Hello,' a female voice answers, 'Brighton Times.'

I steel my shoulders back, faking confidence even though she can't see me. 'I have a story for you. If you're prepared to pay me for it.'

'Okay,' I hear her scrambling around for a pen. 'Can you tell me a few more details?'

'It's about the Mayor of Clayton and his secret illegitimate daughter.'

There's a pause. 'Ooh. And do you have any proof of this?'

'I do. I'm that daughter.'

To say she was interested in my juicy story was an understatement. I told her everything with the promise of her sending me a cheque for five hundred pounds. That money will finally get Mum and the ugly stepsisters off my back for the broken ceiling. After that I don't have to ever see them again.

Thursday 31st August

I can't help that I miss the psycho, can I? Well, I bloody do. So, I've decided that in order to distract myself I'm going to go see Nan. I've been really slacking on seeing her. We still chat every few days on the phone, but it's not the same.

She's asleep when I go into her room. I sit down on the chair next to her bed and watch her sleeping peacefully. She might have a fair few wrinkles, but she still has the longest, darkest eyelashes you've ever seen in your life.

Nan stirs, opening her eyes slowly. Then she opens her mouth and screams.

'Aagh!!!' she yelps, almost jumping out of bed. She stops when she spots it's me, attempting to calm herself down. 'Brooke, you nearly gave me a heart attack!'

I laugh so hard, I clutch at my sides. Only my nan can ever make me laugh this hard.

'Sorry, Nan! God, I was just waiting for you to wake up.'

She sits up, propping the pillow up behind her. 'Well don't watch me sleep like some kind of weird predator. I could have ninja kicked you.'

I burst out laughing again. 'Nan, you're so not a ninja!'

She scoffs. 'You haven't seen me lately. I've been taking the tai chi class here. My legs have always been strong, but now they're amazing. Geoff from down the hall's been commenting on them in the breakfast line. Horny little bastard.'

I can't help but snort out another chuckle. 'Nan!'

This is why I love her so much. She's completely unshockable.

'It's true,' she chortles. 'Anyway, what have you been up to? You look troubled.'

The minute she looks at me with those concerned eyes I can feel myself crumble. I take a deep breath, desperately trying to pull myself back from the edge.

'I'm fine,' I shrug vaguely, trying not to look at her. If I do, I know the pressure will build and I'll burst into tears.

I glance back at her to see her shooting me a look that says, *really?* Dammit, that woman knows me better than anyone.

I roll my eyes. 'Okay fine. I was sort of seeing this guy, but... I'm not anymore.'

'But you still like him?' She smiles knowingly. 'I can tell.'

I shrug. 'It'll never work, Nan. He's far too jealous and possessive.'

She laughs. 'Your grandad was very jealous and possessive. People look at that nowadays like it's a bad thing. Back in my day that just showed he loved you.'

I roll my eyes. 'Yeah, well nowadays it just screams stalker.'

'Is it really that bad?' she asks seriously, her brows

knitted together. 'For a man to be so head over heels in love with you that he can't bear the thought of losing you?'

I swallow the lump in my throat. 'He's not in love with me, Nan.' I take a second to think about it. 'I mean, yeah, if you think about his actions you could think that. But people don't fall in love that quickly nowadays.'

'They do,' she nods knowingly, tutting at me like I'm an idiot. 'Love is the one thing left in this modern world that you still can't control. You young people might try to hide it, but it still happens.'

I sigh, the weight of the whole thing hanging heavily on my shoulders. 'I'm possibly the worst person for him to be with though. You know how I'm flirty and don't like to be tied down. And... well, I like sex a bit too much.'

Nan laughs. Most nan's would be horrified to hear that from their granddaughters. Not mine.

'Enjoying sex is nothing to be ashamed of, Brooke. And I'm pleased you've experienced several men. Variety is the spice of life.'

I put my head in my hands. 'Oh my god, Nan! Stop being so gross.'

'Just because I'm a nan doesn't mean I'm a prude. I was courted by a fair few men before I met your grandad. And I'm glad I did.'

'Nan, stop! I cannot think of you having sex. It's too

weird.'

'Nothing weird about the sexual act, Brooke. It's a beautiful thing when done with the right person.' I cringe, my hands over my eyes. 'But what I really want to know is why you're so scared of a relationship?'

I smile sadly. 'You know I don't want to turn into Mum.'

She shakes her head. 'Don't say that. Your mum is a completely different person to you. Being in a relationship doesn't have to be stifling. It doesn't have to be all consuming. The best partnership makes you feel like a better version of yourself. It doesn't feel like you're giving up anything. When you find that, you need to grab hold of it with both hands.'

She makes it all sound so easy. But she doesn't know I've fucked it all up, anyway.

'Maybe you're right. But what if I've done something unforgivable?'

She smiles sadly, reaching out to stroke my cheek. 'Nothing is unforgiveable. Forgiving is the choice of the person. How do you know unless you give them the chance?'

Can I really give Nicholas the chance to forgive me? Not just from what he thought I'd done, but from what I actually did do? I just don't know if I'm special enough to be forgiven for something reeking so badly of betrayal.

Chapter 17

Friday 1st September

Tonight is Alice's photography exhibition she roped us all into attending. She's invited the whole gang, but I don't know specifically if Nicholas is coming. I haven't heard from him since that day I went off on him. Maybe I damaged him that day.

I still feel awful for that. But he's probably moved on by now. I just hope he doesn't appear with a date. That would truly finish me off.

I can't help but wonder about what Nan said. Should I give him the chance to forgive me? Or is the nicest thing to do to let him go? Let him find some meek girlfriend who'll follow him around like a lost little puppy dog.

So, in preparation I get my eyebrows waxed. I want to look as hot as possible. On the way home, I stop for a quick sunbed session. I haven't had one in a while and I miss the heat on my face. God knows this summer is turning out to be another British washout.

As I get back into my car, I can't help but feel a bit stingy around my eyes. I wonder if it's because they want to cry again. God know I've been doing enough of that lately. They start to stream water involuntarily instead. What the hell? I don't normally get hay fever and I don't feel overly emotional right now. Could I have developed hay fever?

I look into my rearview mirror and my heart misses a beat. My eyes are swollen, red and blotchy. Shit. What happened? And by the looks of it they're increasing in size. What the hell have I done to myself? I must be allergic to something.

What have I eaten in the last few hours? I knew I shouldn't have got that hotdog from the street vendor outside the office. I bet he doesn't even wash his hands after peeing. And now I feel sick too.

I speed home, hiding my face from people with my hair as I run into the flat. I grab some frozen peas from the freezer and place them over my eyes. That feels better. I hear high heels enter the flat. It must be Erica unless Jack has a secret he wants to hide.

'Brooke? What's wrong?'

I remove the peas to explain but she jumps, her face contorting and her eyes nearly popping out of their sockets.

'Shit, what have you done to yourself?' she shrieks.

Way to be supportive Erica. Just what I need right now. Can't she see I'm having a crisis?

'I've no idea.' I throw myself down on the chair in the kitchen, holding my head in my hands. 'This morning I got my eyebrows waxed and then had a sunbed and next thing I know I look like I've been punched. I think it was a bad hotdog reaction.'

'Shit, maybe that's why,' she nods, around her eyes creased in thought. 'Don't they tell you not to have any hot baths after waxing?'

I shake my head in confusion. 'Yeah, so?'

'So maybe it's because of the heat or something? Like the sunbed has reacted with it and caused this rash?'

Oh God. Could that really be it?

'Shit, that does sound plausible. What the hell am I going to do? The exhibition is tonight!'

She takes a deep breath as if she's the worried one.

'Don't panic. We'll just carry on icing them for the rest of the day and worst-case scenario I'll give you some smoky eyes with my eyeshadow palette.'

Oh God, I'm going to look like a bloody monster.

'Okay,' I nod, taking deep breaths to try to calm myself down. Thank the Lord above for make-up. 'Just please tell me Nicholas isn't coming tonight?'

She grimaces, baring her teeth. 'All the boys are coming down. They're already at the Holiday Inn.'

Shit. Just how I want to see him after all this time. Looking like a big swollen fish.

My eyes have gone down, thank God. But not quite back to normal. They're still puffy so Erica spent over twenty minutes giving me smoky grey eyes while simultaneously watching a YouTube video on how to do it. I'm not filled with confidence.

I look in the mirror. To be truthful, I'm not sure if it looks better or worse, but after all her care and attention I don't want to upset her. Besides, wearing this amazing dress I treated myself to, people should be looking at that and the way it clings to my body, not my face.

We're meeting the others there which has given me a chance to have three mini panic attacks and one tantrum where I threatened to not go at all. Erica's told me in no uncertain terms that I'm not backing out. Jack's said he feels like he's dealing with Esme. Being compared to a four-year-old really forced me to pull myself together.

Whatever. We're going to show support for Alice. I'm actually interested to see her work. I don't keep up with her Facebook page and she's always shy as fuck about showing off her stuff.

If I had a skill like that I'd be showing it to anyone that'd look. I mean, Jesus, look how many people I show my cooch to and that can't even be referred to as a skill. Although if it was, I'd obviously have the fucking Olympic gold medal.

As I walk into the vast hall with Jack and Erica, I can't help but feel like a nervous schoolgirl. God, this whole dating is just so bloody awkward. No wonder I've avoided it for so long. Mindless sex is much easier.

At least I know I look banging in this dress. I still can't believe I ever bought it. It was over a grand in one of those small boutiques that only sells one off dresses. I swear, I thought the shop assistant was going to come over and claim "we don't have anything for you", Pretty Woman style. I stuck it on the credit card but I have a plan. I just have to make sure that I don't spill anything on it and then I can return it tomorrow. I don't think I'm even going to drink that much. It'll just affect my judgement and I can't afford to lose that money.

I take a glass of champagne from the tray of a passing waitress and scan the room. Molly spots me, looking absolutely gorgeous in a peach floor-length dress with ruffles on the top half. It's so bloody girly, but it suits her down to the ground.

She sees us and practically skips over.

'Hey, guys,' she says giving me a kiss on the cheek. 'Wow, Brooke, that dress!'

I smile, doing a little twirl for her. See, she understands why I had to buy it. It's a low-cut slip dress with spaghetti straps and has sequinned detailing on the hips which runs down the length of the floor-length skirt.

'Why, thank you.'

I needed that compliment. It's far too skimpy to wear any underwear so I'm very conscious of my erect nipples. That along with my swollen eyes has me feeling like an insecure little bitch.

'Where's Alice?' Erica asks, looking around for her.

Alice suddenly runs over, grabbing my champagne out of my hand and necking it. 'I'm so bloody nervous.'

'Don't be,' I reassure her, rubbing her back. It reminds me of Nicholas. He used to rub my back. I shake the thought out of my head. 'If you should be nervous of anything it's me decking you for stealing my champers.'

She cringes and it's only then I notice she's visibly shaking. Jesus, how worried is she? It's just a load of pictures. It's not like she has to stand up naked and do a speech or anything. Unless this is really one of those weird arty events you hear about.

'Look around,' I smile reassuringly, 'the place looks amazing!' And it does. The conference hall is decorated with candles, and art work from local artists which has totally brightened the usually bland place up. I just wonder which are hers.

She grins wide. 'I just hope somebody buys some paintings tonight. Otherwise it's all just a waste of time.'

Me and Erica exchange rolled eyes.

'Or,' Erica says, 'it's a great way to showcase your talent.'

'Whatever,' she shrugs. 'If I have to go photograph another wedding I'll just die.'

I nod, not really knowing what she's going on about. Weddings can't be that bad, right? I bet she gets loads of free booze and access to fit men.

Tom's booming laugh from behind interrupts us. I swing round to see the lads coming in. My God, Nicholas looks fucking edible. He's wearing a navy suit and a white shirt done up to the top with no tie. On closer inspection, it's one of those grandad collars. Only he could pull off something like that, his neck tattoos spilling free from it.

I look away quickly and neck Erica's glass of champagne. Shit, I'm not supposed to be drinking loads. I look down at the dress. Mustn't get shit-faced. Must protect the dress.

I can feel him here, like every hair on my body is standing proud, desperate to make contact with him. God, why is my body so traitorous? It's always been a needy slut.

'Hey.' It's him, his dulcet tones forcing me to close my eyes. I've wanted so badly to hear that voice for so long, but in reality it brings with it so many more heart-stopping feelings.

I turn to see him holding two glasses of champagne, staring at me intently.

'Hi,' I mumble. God, I can't look him in the eye. Last time I saw him I was such an unnecessary bitch.

The others quickly make themselves scarce. He hands one of the glasses to me. Why on earth is he being so nice to me? I take it with a polite smile.

'I can't stand this fucking bubbly stuff,' he says, as if forcing himself to make polite conversation. 'Give me a Jack and coke any day.'

I smile, pleased at his attempt to break the ice. 'Me too.'

I rock on my heels. Oh God, I have to bring it up. This is excruciating.

'Listen, about what happened...'

'Don't worry,' he interrupts, shaking his head as if it was no big deal. As if I didn't witness the pain in those midnight blue eyes.

'No, please let me say it,' I insist. I take a deep breath, attempting to collect my scattered thoughts. 'Look, I was a total bitch to you and I had no right. I'm sorry.'

'It's cool,' he nods. I don't miss the bob of his Adam's apple as he gulps.

'I couldn't stop myself from getting so angry. And I have to know. Did you shag that skank?'

His eyes nearly bulge out of their sockets.

'Oh my God, no.' He steps forward and for a second I think he's going to take me into his arms. I hold my breath in anticipation, but he stops himself, instead running his hand through his hair. 'I was totally hammered. Tom took me out to try to cheer me up and the next thing I knew she was sat on my lap. Then you were there.'

'Anyway,' I interrupt, not wanting to think of that night any longer than I had to. 'It's all probably for the best.'

He holds my stare, his eyes like ice. 'That's where you're wrong, Brooke. Me and you *will* happen. If I have to keep apologising every time I see you that's fine. I'm willing to do it, but the end game is that I have to have you.'

Wow. Good speech. *Really* good speech.

'You've already had me,' I say with a nervous laugh, trying to break the intense tension.

He shakes his head, no humour in his face.

'No. I need you to be mine. Fully, no crap. Just us.'

I smile, but it's taken from me when I remember the night I ran to Simon's hotel room. The way I doubted him so quickly. Shit, we're both such fuck ups. This will never work.

'Can we go for a walk outside?' I ask, attempting to have courage.

I need to tell him. Even if he rightly tells me what a horrid slut I am and says he never wants to see me again. At least then he can stop lusting after me and stop these thoughts of us ending happily ever after.

He nods, taking my hand and leading me towards the patio doors. God, just having his hand in mine is enough to make me dizzy. What is it about him that turns me so crazy and unstable?

We walk through the outside gardens, the view of the distant beach breathtaking. I turn to him before it starts getting too romantic.

'Listen, Nicholas. I have to tell you something.'

Here goes. I look into his blue eyes lit up by the moonlight, aware I'm potentially about to break his heart.

He takes my other hand and pulls me closer to him.

'What were you trying to say?'

'Oh, I-'

He smiles, and it's so beautiful I have to remind myself why I'm trying to ruin this.

So, what if he doesn't know about that night? The main thing is that we're trying again. Starting afresh. That we want each other.

Is it really worth throwing away a potentially great relationship because of one really stupid decision?

'I just... wanted to ask if we could have a fresh start?'

He smiles, taking me around the waist, sending tingles up and down my spine. 'Here's to our fresh start.'

'Fresh start,' I nod.

He leans forward to kiss the corner of my mouth before placing his mouth fully on my lips as if it's always belonged there. His hand travels up my spine until it's in my hair, sliding out to frame my jaw.

He pushes his tongue past my lips, claiming my mouth possessively. God, is it wrong that I love how possessive he is over me?

He breaks the kiss only to pull me against his chest, his arms encased around me. It's weird, but I never thought a hug could feel so good.

We walk back into the hall hand in hand just as our gang is crowded around a photo. Nicholas leads me over towards them, his hand on my lower back. I love how he always feels the need to touch me.

I look up at the huge canvas and realise that it's a picture of Erica lying on a sunbed. Alice must have taken it at Luna Island. As I look closer, I notice she's glancing over to Jack in the distance who's also looking at her. They both have this agonised expression on their faces. It's as if you can feel the longing between them. It's beautiful.

'When did you even take this?' Erica asks Alice who's going as red as a beetroot. 'I didn't think you brought your camera away with us.'

'I took it with my iPhone,' she admits shyly. 'Truthfully, I didn't even plan on showing it but the organisers loved it. Apparently there are already a few bids on it.'

'You're joking,' Erica gasps, astounded.

I burst out laughing. 'Jack, how do you feel about Erica's tits being in someone else's house?'

He frowns. 'Fuck that.' He storms off towards the bidding desk.

'It really is stunning,' Nicholas muses out loud.

'Now, now,' I joke, pinching his bum, 'you'll have me getting jealous.'

He grins back at me. 'And I thought I was the jealous and possessive one.'

I feel a little faint at how he's looking at me. Like the world stops and ends with me.

Jack reappears looking a little beaten. 'That photo is being sold for over three thousand quid!'

Alice's mouth drops open. 'Shit.'

Molly raises her glass of champagne. 'I think that means we should all get drunk to celebrate! Here's to Alice.'

Chapter 18

Friday 1st September continued

Nicholas and I make it back to the flat at about one am. I'm still relatively sober and my dress is stain free. After how hard we celebrated I've no idea how I've managed it. I still can't believe how much everyone loved Alice's photography. She sold all of her pictures. She won't be doing weddings for a long time.

I put the keys onto our hallway table. He slides up behind me, pushing my hair to one side so he can kiss my neck. I'm turned around and my back is slammed against the wall.

His lips kiss me with such force I actually forget who I am for a moment, all my thoughts scatter. All I can do is revel in his kisses and the feelings they incite, my skin tingling all over.

I force myself to break away, conscious of having to remove all this eye make-up before it makes my eyes even worse. I don't want to terrify him in the morning.

'You go through to my room. I'll just go take my make-up off.'

He frowns, as if confused that I'd be more interested in getting ready for bed than shagging him. Which, you know, is really unusual for me, but I need a minute. Plus, I want to feel comfortable when I jump him. Knowing my luck, I'd rip the dress when taking it off.

I go into the bathroom and lift up my sea-green Borghese make-up remover. I only bought it the other day after reading rave reviews from my favourite make-up blogger and today is the perfect day to try it out. So I grab a piece of cotton wool and press down on the pump. It shoots out straight onto my dress, right at my heart.

I stumble and gasp as if I've been shot. No. No! I can't afford this dress! I've made it all fucking night and *now* I ruin it? It's a grand!

I stumble down the corridor and into my bedroom.

Nicholas looks up from where he's sitting on the bed unbuttoning his shirt. I stagger in, clutching my chest, eyes wide in horror.

His mouth drops open. 'Shit, what's happened?' He rushes over to me, peeling my hand away. His eyes scrunch closed in confusion when he spots the green smudge. 'This is... just some cream?'

What, did he think I was really shot or something?

'You don't understand. This dress costs a grand! I still have the tags on. I was planning on returning it tomorrow.'

He frowns, narrowing his eyes at me. 'So, you bought a dress you couldn't afford?'

'Duh!' I snap, grabbing a towel and trying desperately to remove the mess as best I can. It only seems to smear it around. Shit.

I take it off, hanging it back up, praying to God it'll dry back to perfect. Miracles do happen, right?

He smiles, his eyes raking over my completely naked body with a greedy hunger in them.

'Come here,' he demands, reaching his arms out to me.

I've never wanted to run into someone's arms so much before.

I walk slowly towards him, revelling in the power of delaying it. His eyes hood over, his dick straining in his trousers. I stand between his legs. He grabs my waist and within a second has thrown me onto the bed and is towering above me.

I love how he throws me around with no fear of hurting me. He grabs one of my tits, forcing the other into his mouth. He bites down hard; so hard I yelp. It's instantly replaced with his tongue lapping at it in soothing circles.

He growls. 'God, I love that you've been completely naked underneath that all night.' He gazes into my eyes, his own alight with hunger.

'Just shut up and fuck me.'

He barks out a laugh. 'You're so romantic.'

He takes hold of my legs and yanks them apart roughly. He slinks down there, taunting me with his eyes. What is he going to do?

He licks from my belly button all the way down to my fully waxed vajayjay. He stops to suck my clit. I hiss out, not used to anyone paying me this much attention. Normally it's wham bam, thank you ma'am.

He locks eyes with me as I lean up on my elbows to watch him. It's beyond hot. He lingers his tongue down to my opening, using his two index fingers to part me. God, this is weird.

Then his mouth is on me again, whirling his tongue around, like he's licking the last few drops of ice cream from his sundae. Wow, it feels divine. I grasp the bed sheets, feeling as if I need to centre myself so I don't actually float up to the ceiling.

'Stop,' I moan, unable to take it. It's like being tickled in the most intimate part of my body. Unbearable and delicious.

He lifts his head, a hungry grin on his face, as he rises back up to kiss me, pulling his trousers and boxers down. He shifts his weight to one side to use his other hand to line himself up against me. A second later he slips inside me slowly, his shirt still on.

Dear God, it's like the sweetest kind of agony.

He scrunches his eyes shut and takes a breath, leaning his forehead against mine.

'Move,' I beg, stroking his back with my nails.

He starts thrusting into me, slowly at first, but building up to a steady rhythm, every thrust jolting me up towards my headrest.

Every spare moment he has he's kissing me, licking me, even nipping on my ear lobes. It's beyond hot.

His thrusts grow more urgent, his eyes crinkled in the corners with effort. Suddenly they're open, his teeth biting into his lower lip.

He clasps his hands around my neck, applying pressure. Shit, he's choking me? He's pressing enough that I can still breathe, but I can't take a deep inhale of breath. I'd be worried if I wasn't about to come like a freight train.

My whole body tingles, a pressure building not only in my lungs but in my stomach. I squeeze my legs around him, needing the increased pressure. He shifts, taking me with him, moving so my head is hanging off the bed. All the blood rushes to my head as he pounds into me urgently.

Something explodes inside me sending me soaring up to the ceiling, a feeling of total euphoria settling over my tense muscles. He grunts, collapsing down on top of me.

Dear. God.

Why have we waited this long to have sex?

I gently push him off me, needing to breathe. He moves himself next to me, reaching out and wrapping his arm around my stomach.

'That was amazing,' I pant, still out of breath.

He smiles lazily up at me. 'It really was.'

I relax into his hold for what feels like twenty minutes. When I start to feel my eyelids dragging themselves closed, I remind myself that I have to take this eye make up off or my eyes are going to be in even worse condition in the morning.

I drag myself out of bed and make my way to the bathroom to remove all the smoky eyeshadow. They're still slightly swollen, but I'm confident he won't notice.

I make my way back into the room, making myself comfortable in the bed.

He turns to me, his face contorted. 'Jesus, B, what the hell have you done to your eyes?'

Okay. Maybe they're still *slightly* noticeable.

Saturday 2nd September

I wake up to him bringing me breakfast in bed, his muscled tattooed legs the first thing I see. I could seriously get used to this scenario.

'God, you're the best.'

He grins, that delicious smile reserved only for me. It makes me want to peel his boxer shorts off and give him a blowie to thank him just for existing.

'I was thinking we'd eat this and then go have a coffee on the beach.'

I raise my eyebrows. 'Are you starting to come around to Brighton?'

He rolls his eyes. 'I'm not saying I want to move here or anything, but it's growing on me.'

It makes me wonder what the hell we're going to do. Why in the hell did I want to fall for someone who lives so far away? I need to address it if we're really together now.

'So... are you cool with us going back and forth between Peterborough and here?' I ask, tearing off some of my croissant and stuffing it in my mouth to stop myself from rambling further.

'You could always move to Peterborough with me?' he asks, appearing nonplussed, but I can hear the hopefulness behind it.

How crazy is he? We've been together five minutes, and he's talking about me moving to his home town.

The thought of having to leave Brighton behind and move to that A road maze has my stomach churning. And leaving my girls behind? I couldn't do it.

'Sorry, but I don't think I could ever live there,' I admit with a sad smile. 'I love Brighton so much. It's my home now.'

He smiles sadly. 'Well I can't move here while my dad's recovering. He doesn't have anyone else, you know? And if he's gonna be ill with his health, I want to spend as much time with him as possible. You understand that, right?'

'Of course,' I nod.

And I do. It just totally sucks for us. He could live for another thirty years for all we know.

'But, I mean, you'll be okay with that, right? You won't get mad jealous knowing I'm here and you're there?'

He smiles, a real smile, showing off his perfect teeth. 'I can't promise that, but I trust you, Brooke.'

I smile back, feeling the crushing guilt make itself home on my chest. I don't deserve his trust. I should confess right here and now. But instead I smile pushing it back down until it's making my gut churn and take a sip of my coffee.

We've just got our coffees from Costa and are walking hand in hand towards the beach. I feel so proud to have him on my arm. I notice a few frisky bitches give him the once over, clearly appreciating his gorgeousness. He's mine. The thought has me beaming. This must be what it feels like to be possessive.

But more than any of that I feel happy. Just simply happy.

We're almost at the beach when I spot Simon. Shit. My stomach contracts in fear. I quickly look down, eager not to catch his eye. He *cannot* see me. If Nicholas finds out, it'll ruin everything.

I glance back up quickly and see that he's with his nutcase of a wife. Shit. Please God, don't let them see me.

I attempt to cover my face with my hair and look towards Nicholas. He smiles at me, clearly having no idea of the shit show that could potentially happen any second.

'I don't believe it,' a female voice shrieks.

Oh God, it's her. The wife. I know it is.

I make the mistake of glancing up and find her standing in front of me, glaring daggers.

'Well, well, well,' she says, arms crossed over her

chest, 'If it isn't the little tramp.'

I glance to see Nicholas' reaction. He turns to look at me with raised eyebrows, obviously expecting me to be wondering who this nutter is. It quickly changes to a frown. He turns back to the wife, his fists clenching.

'Sorry, but who the hell are you?' he asks her aggressively. I love that he feels the need to jump to my defence. If only I deserved it.

Simon's behind her looking mortified. He bloody should. He never told me he was married. That part at least is on him.

'I'm the *wife* of the man she's been shagging!'

Nicholas turns to look at me in disbelief, rubbing his forehead. 'What's she talking about?'

I shake my head, desperately wanting to grab him and run away. 'Nothing.'

I really should run for it, but it's like my entire body has shut down and gone into self-preservation mode.

Simon walks in front of her, an apologetic smile on his face. 'Sorry, Brooke. I had no idea she was following me the other night.'

I try to communicate with wide eyes for him to shut the fuck up. Can't he see that this is my guy?

'The other night?' Nicholas repeats, searching for understanding between our faces. 'What other night?'

Oh God, why is this happening to me?

Simon's eyes widen, finally catching on. 'Shit, are you Brooke's boyfriend? Sorry, I didn't mean to cause any trouble.'

'Bit too late for that,' his wife snorts, turning on her heel and flouncing off. Finally.

Simon quickly follows her. Leaving me to try to explain this. Where the fuck am I going to start?

I take a discreet deep breath before turning to look at Nicholas. His face has paled, his mouth slack. But his eyes; they hold so much betrayal it's hard to look at him. I've never seen someone look so disappointed in all of my life.

'What the fuck, Brooke?' he asks, his voice almost a whisper.

'I... I'm so sorry.' It's all I can say. All I want to say. The worst thing to do would be to lie further right now.

'You were with him the other night?' he asks, repulsion clear in his features.

I bite down on my lip. 'Well... yes, but not like that.'

'So, you didn't fuck him?' he asks, his eyes blazed with a fresh bout of rage.

'No, but...' I look down at the ground, hanging my head in shame. How can I say I just started giving him a blowie?

He nods, as if understanding. 'But you were going to until his wife busted in?'

I hunch my shoulders, so ashamed I wish I could melt into the floor. 'Yes. But you don't understand. I thought you'd dumped me.'

I look up to see his face change in recognition.

'So, my dad was lying in hospital and you thought because you hadn't heard from me that you'd go shag some random.'

'He's not some random. We've been shagging for months.'

Oh God, why the fuck did I say that? I was trying to make myself seem less slutty, that I didn't just pick up a guy in a bar, but this is far worse.

'What. The. Fuck.' His eyes protrude, his nostrils flaring.

Okay, that couldn't have gone worse. 'Not like that. I mean, not really since we started this thing between us.'

'Ha!' he scoffs, his eyes tight. 'Don't make it sound like we're exclusive, Brooke. Apparently, you have no idea what that means.'

Ouch, that hurts.

He turns away from me, storming off. I'd chase him if I thought I'd have any chance of making things better. Instead I watch as my happiness leaves with him.

Chapter 19

Monday 4th September

Devastation is an understatement. I never knew when I'd met him on Luna Island that I'd end up so infatuated with him that if he ever left my life, I'd feel empty. It's crazy how I've come to rely on having him around in such a short space of time.

I've been thinking about it and although he may never forgive me, I have to try to beg for his forgiveness. I won't rest until I've at least tried. The only thing I can think of is by doing some kind of grand gesture. It always works in the movies, right?

Except I've come up blank. I mean, in real life what can you do without looking like a crazy stalker bitch? I can't turn up outside his house with a boom box blaring. There's no time to learn the guitar and pen him a romantic ballad. What does that leave me with?

The saying *if you love them let them go* keeps

running over any of my potential plans. I keep pushing it out. First of all, I'd have to decide if I actually loved him. I have no idea as I've never been in love before. I mean, yeah, I love my nan, but I've never been "in love" with anyone. So, I have no idea what it feels like, apart from again, what I've seen in movies and what I've heard in love songs.

All I know is that I have an empty longing in my chest and every time I think about us not ending up together I feel sick with weighted dread.

Erica comes in while I'm sat at the kitchen table contemplating it all.

'Hey, B,' she says, carrying in a bag full of groceries. 'How you feeling?'

When we left each other this morning I still had puffy eyes from crying so much last night.

'Fine,' I insist, forcing a cheery smile.

She raises her eyebrows in disbelief. 'I'm not an idiot, Brooke.' She folds her arms over her chest. 'I get that you fucked up, but I really think you need to fight to get him back.'

'I've already thought of that, but God knows what I can do to make it up to him. It's not exactly like I can just send an *I'm Sorry* card.'

'Brooke, if you love the guy, you'll find a way.'

I roll my eyes. 'That's the thing. I don't know if I am

in love with him. I mean, how do you know?'

She smiles knowingly. 'I suppose the way I realised was when the thought of not being with him made me feel physically ill. I just... I love Jack to bits. Sorry, I don't really know how to put the feeling into words.'

'Well that's helpful,' I deadpan with a smile.

She laughs. 'Well if it helps, you totally look like a loved-up puppy dog. Or smitten kitten. Giddy guinea pig.' She creases over laughing as if she's hysterical.

I can't help but laugh with her. 'Okay, but what do you think I should do to win him back? Some kind of grand gesture?'

She bites her lip, frowning as if deep in thought. 'I'm not sure if an empty gesture would work with Nicholas. You need something that he really cares about. Something he'd maybe be too proud to do himself?'

That's when it pops into my head. His mum. He said himself that everyone leaves a paper trail. I bet I could track her down. He acts like he doesn't care, but I know that he does, that it kills him to think of his mum getting up and leaving them both. He'd be too proud to go after her. To even find out where she is. But I can. I can find out where she is and if she regretted giving him up.

'I've got it,' I smile to Erica, a new spring in my step.

'What?' she asks, clapping her hands excitedly.

'I can't tell you, but it's awesome.'

She shakes her head slightly. I don't care. I'm already typing into my laptop.

Okay, this could be a bit of a nightmare. I don't even know the woman's name. Just that her surname is Parker. Hopefully his dad would have filed a missing person's report.

I put Parker mother missing Peterborough in my search engine. It's bound to bring up something. *Body of missing woman found in hotel* is the first result. Shit. My blood runs cold. This can't be Nicholas' Mum... right?

I dubiously click on the link. It's from a local paper's website.

Police searching for missing Cynthia Parker have found the body of a woman. The body was discovered at The West & East hotel in Peterborough. Cynthia, 31, went missing from her home in Devon Road, Peterborough, late morning 21st March. The death is not being treated as suspicious.

Shit the bed. I bring up the calculator app on my phone to try to work out dates. The article is dated 1995. Nicholas is twenty-nine. She left when he was seven. Yep, the dates work out. Could this really be her? Without her name and the date she went missing it's impossible to tell.

And what does not treating her death suspiciously mean? Did she die of natural causes? Or... I gulp at the thought; does it mean she committed suicide?

Jack lets himself in the door, going straight to the fridge for a beer. Jack will know. I just have to seem casual.

'Hey Jack. How was work?' I ask, all smiles.

He frowns, clearly suspicious. I suppose I'm not normally this chatty with him.

'Rough,' he admits on a sigh. 'The boss is a fucking arsehole.'

God, who knew? Other people have shit going on in their lives too. When did I become so bloody self-obsessed?

'So... anyway. Random question for you, but what is Nicholas' mum's name?'

He stops dead in his tracks, his eyes darting from side to side. 'Why do you want to know her name?'

I shrug. 'I just do, okay?'

He narrows his eyes at me. 'You're not looking for her, are you?'

I roll my eyes. Interfering bastard. 'Maybe I am. Look, I just want her bloody name. It won't get back to anyone that you helped me out.'

He turns his lip up in doubt. God, you tell a few secrets and people think you're a loudmouthed gossip.

'It's Cynthia.'

Shit. It's her. His mum is dead.

Chapter 20

Tuesday 5th September

I still can't believe it. Nicholas lied to me about his mum going missing. The truth is that she died. Whether it be from taking her own life or maybe dealing with a secret mystery illness, I don't know.

That's how I find myself having told my employers I'm working from home for the day, when instead I'm on my way to Peterborough to confront him about it. The truth is that I do most of my work at night, anyway.

The more I think about it the more I think that Jack and the guys don't know the truth either. I was the way he answered my questions. *She's called Cynthia. Are you looking for her?* It all sounded like he was talking about her in the present tense. If he knew she'd died, he'd have said she *was* called Cynthia.

But that doesn't make sense to me. If it was in the local paper then surely everyone knew? I know the boys were only young, but they also weren't stupid. Unless they completely covered it up and didn't have a funeral, I don't know how else they'd have missed it.

I pull onto his road far too quickly for my liking. By now I was hoping to have some awesome speech planned. Or at least some kind of plan. But I have nothing. Zero. Nada.

I get out of the car slowly, noticing Nicholas' car is outside his house. He's in. Looking at my clock I see that its 2pm. I assumed he'd still be at work.

I force myself to walk to the door, my legs as heavy as timber. It's like they're begging me to turn around and change my mind. But I have to speak to him about it. I don't care how we left things.

I take a deep breath before knocking on the door. Then I tap my foot, pretending to inspect my nails on my shaky hand. I don't want to look as nervous as I feel.

After what feels like an eternity I hear footsteps on the other side of the door. It's opened slowly to reveal Nicholas looking just as devastated as I did this morning. He has dark circles around his eyes, his hair is in disarray as if he's run his hands through it a million times and his shoulders are slumped in defeat. I want to run to him and put my arms around him, but I know he wouldn't want that. He's still too pissed off.

'Hi.' It's pathetic and completely understated in this

whole situation, but it's all I've got right now.

'Hi,' he replies back, looking at me through hooded midnight blue eyes. They communicate so much distress without him saying another word.

'How are you doing?' I ask, biting my lip in anticipation of an answer.

He sighs, running his hand through his already wayward hair. 'How do you think, Brooke?'

It guts me like nothing else. I've caused this hurt. This is all my fault.

'I'm so sorry.' I hang my head in shame. More sorry than he'll ever know. 'Can I come in?'

For a minute, I don't think he's going to let me. He stares at me, his eyes scrutinising my face, trying to work out what my angle is. He eventually nods, standing back to let me in.

I go to walk into the sitting room, but he takes my hand and starts pulling me up the stairs. He wants me upstairs?

He opens the door to his bedroom and sits us down on the edge of his bed.

Then he turns to me. 'I want you to explain it.'

Oh God. He wants all the gory details.

'Okay.' I take a deep breath. 'But are you sure you want to hear it?'

'I'm sure,' he nods.

I gulp. He deserves the truth, but I know this is just going to hurt him further.

'I thought we were together and then I didn't hear from you for days. I got myself all worked up thinking you were just like Tom. Like you were playing me for a bit of fun. I even imagined Tom and you laughing about it together.'

He purses his lips together, fidgeting with the zip of his hoodie.

I force myself to continue. 'Me and the girls went out, and I got ridiculously pissed. The next thing I knew Simon was texting me for a booty call and I just thought why not?'

His face creases in hurt. 'So, you just thought I'd throw away what we had?'

I nod. If only I'd known what we did have when we had it.

'I clearly have trust issues. But it was radio silence your end. I'm not blaming you, obviously. You were dealing with your dad. I'm a slut. I've been shagging Simon on and off for six months. It felt familiar. But I had no idea he had a wife until she stormed in on us in that hotel room.'

He grimaces, the images clearly flashing through his mind. 'Did you sleep with him?' His eyes beg me to tell him the truth, no matter how much harm they cause.

'No.' Thank God, I didn't. 'But...' God, how do I admit this? My upper lip is sweating. 'We did kiss, and I'd started to give him a... blow job.'

I hang my head in shame. Never have I felt such a slag in my entire life. I close my eyes, knowing one way or another he needed to know. He deserves the truth even if it is ugly.

He bends over, his elbows on his knees, head in his hands.

'I know that you probably can't ever forgive me and that's fine.' What am I saying? That's not fine at all. 'But I came here to ask you why you didn't feel like you could tell me about your mum?'

He stares back at me, his eyebrows furrowed. 'You've lost me. Tell you what about my mum?'

My eyes peruse his features, trying to work out if he's lying or if he truly doesn't know.

I stare at him sternly. 'I need you to tell me the truth right now. Do you know more about your mum other than she walked out on you?'

He frowns, itching at his forearms. 'Brooke, you're worrying me. What do you know that I don't?'

Wow. He really doesn't know. How the hell have they hidden this from him?

'So, you've honestly never Googled her before?' I find it hard to believe. I mean, the guy's in IT.

He sighs. 'I told you, why on earth would I want to find out where the woman who willingly left us is? We're the ones that haven't moved this whole time. If she wanted to find us she could. She's obviously moved on.'

Moved on is an understatement. Moved on to an afterlife.

This is horrendous. How am I going to break this to him?

He clenches his jaw. 'What do you know, Brooke?'

I take a deep breath. He deserves to know. 'Okay, I looked her up and... well, the internet says that she... died.'

He stares back at me completely flummoxed. 'Died? When?'

Oh God, he must think I mean in the last couple of years. I swallow the lump in my throat. 'Only a day after leaving you. In your local hotel.'

His eyes dance from side to side before he jumps up to standing. 'No.' He shakes his head. 'You must have got it wrong. My mum left. She left a note for Dad.'

I twist my hands awkwardly in my lap. 'It was in the paper.' I take the printed sheet out of my pocket and unfold it, handing it over.

He takes it from me, his eyes quickly scanning over the contents. It's hardly a large article, just a paragraph, but it still has him staring at it repeatedly. 'This has to be wrong.'

I nod. 'I hope it is.'

My phone starts ringing. I look down at it, ready to reject whoever is trying to get hold of me, when I see it's my nan's home calling. Shit. It might be Nan urgently needing to speak to me.

'Sorry, I just have to get this quickly.' I answer it. 'Hello?'

'Miss Archer?'

'Yes.' Dread settles into my gut. 'What's wrong? Is it my nan?'

'I'm afraid she's got a chest infection and has taken quite poorly. She's requested for you to come in.'

Oh my God.

'Shit. Is she okay? Does she need to go to the hospital?'

'We're treating her in-house for now. She should be fine, but she requested me to call you specifically.'

Crap. If she asked for them to call me that means she's scared. And this is Nan. She's never frightened. I've never seen her afraid my whole entire life. Once when I was fifteen, we thought someone had broken in. Even then, as she was holding the hoover nozzle over her head as a weapon she didn't have an ounce of fear in her face. Just an angry, determined gaze ready to beat the potential robber to death. It was just my mum letting herself in while drunk.

And right now when she needs me I'm in bloody Peterborough.

'I'm in Peterborough right now but I'll be there as soon as the traffic will let me. Please tell her I love her and I'll be there as soon as I can.'

I turn back to Nicholas. He keeps looking between the letter and me. He has enough to worry about right now.

'Just speak to your dad. I have to go see my nan.'

Nicholas

I feel awful not having run out after Brooke, but it's like my legs won't work. My Mum... dead? It's too hard to believe. I've spent my entire life feeling angry and resentful whenever I've thought of her. And now I find out she might not have left us at all. She might have died. Be looking down at me as I curse her to hell.

I need to know. While I've been waiting for Dad to get home, I've pulled out the old family albums and gone through all the pictures taken before her death. She doesn't look ill. I can't see any signs of her having lost her hair or appearing paler than normal.

Then I think of my other conclusion. Could she

really have ended her life on purpose? She's smiling in the photos, but then I suppose you don't normally get the camera out when you're bursting into tears.

I hear Dad's van park up outside. This is it. Now or never.

'Nicholas?' he calls as soon as he's inside. 'How are you feeling?'

I told him I was sick, so he didn't bitch at me for not going into work.

I walk down the stairs, unsure of how to start this conversation. He's in the kitchen filling up the kettle. Instead of talking I put the print out down in front of him.

He picks it up, frowning at me, before putting his reading glasses on and looking over the words. His face pales immediately.

'Where did you get this?' he asks, looking at me in disbelief.

'Forget where I got it from. Is it true?'

He falls back against the worktop. Shit. Am I bringing on another heart attack bringing this up? I rush over to him. 'Dad, are you okay?'

'I... I just need to sit down.'

I lead him into the sitting room and sit him down on the sofa.

'Shall I call someone?' Maybe he needs to go back to the hospital for a check-up.

'I'm fine,' he insists.

'I need the truth, Dad.'

'It's true,' he nods, his eyes glassy with unshed tears. 'Your mother passed.'

An all-consuming grief settles over my heart like a black veil.

'Then why the fuck did you tell me she left us? Leave me pissed at her for all these years?'

'I'm sorry Nic, but we thought it was for the best.'

'We? Who the fuck is we?' I bark, my voice breaking slightly.

He sighs, putting his head into his hands. 'All of us. Me, your uncle, your friend's parents. You were just a little boy, Nicholas. How was I supposed to tell you that your mum had died?'

'So instead you decided to tell me she left me instead?' I can't help but sound accusatory.

He scratches his forehead. 'I intended to tell you. But time went on and there never seemed a good time to tell you. So... well, we decided to just keep up the lie.'

'So, what? The whole town decided to keep it a secret from me?'

'Not just from you, Nic, from everyone. All of your friends believe that's what happened too.'

Well, that's something at least. The thought of them all knowing and keeping it a secret from me had me wanting to punch them in the face.

'But why? It can't just be because you wanted to spare my feelings. I would have gotten over it, eventually.' I frown.

'Nic, you don't understand. The way she died...'

'She took her own life, didn't she?' I interrupt, having no time for niceties. He looks down at the floor. 'Didn't she?!' I roar, jumping to my feet.

He nods. 'She did. Your mother, she'd suffered from depression since you were born. It wasn't like it is nowadays. Suicide was a huge taboo back then. I didn't want to put you through that.'

'So instead you had me grow up thinking I wasn't important enough for my mother not to abandon me?'

'I did what I felt was right at the time. I'm so sorry, son. But you have to understand that I was also grieving my wife. I loved your mother more than anything and I always will.'

He reaches up to a vase on the top of our display cabinet and produces some paper from it. 'This was her note. Read it in your own time.'

I open up the letter. It's so old the edges where it's been folded have faded some of the writing. I know it to be my mum's handwriting from the birthday cards Dad kept.

My darling son,

I'm so sorry for having to leave you, my baby boy, but I must leave this cruel world. I know you'll be looked after, left in the capable hands of your loving father. Just know that I didn't do this because I didn't love you. I did this because I do love you. You deserve better than for me to mess up your life. You deserve the world, my darling boy.

I hope that when you grow up, you'll find someone who makes you happy. I hope she isn't weak like me. You need a strong girl to help fight your battles, to be in your corner and to love you with every inch of her heart.

That is the very least you deserve, my darling boy. I will be watching over you, trying to guide you in the decisions you make. Just please remember that I love you and that I am safe now. I'm with Grandma and Grandad.

I'm sorry I couldn't stay.

All my love, forever, Mum xxx

Chapter 21

Brooke

Friday 8th September

When I got to Nan on Tuesday night, she was weak and tired, but the nurse assured me she was on the road to recovery. Instead of being worried a strange kind of rage has overtaken me instead. If she, God forbid, were to die I wouldn't have anyone. I was living with the hope that I could someday rely on my dad. The guy I was hanging all hopes on being a good guy. Only now I know he's a dickhead who didn't want me and never does want me.

Plus, I haven't heard anything from Nicholas since last night. I'm dying to know what his dad said when he confronted him, but I doubt he'll want to tell me. Typical of me to destroy the one good thing I had going for me.

Today is the day the article on my dad comes out.

Now that it's actually going to be out there I can't help but feel extremely nervous. I mean, I've potentially ruined his whole family dynamic because I'm pissed he abandoned me.

But no, I must remember he *did* abandon me. I shouldn't feel guilty about it. I tracked him down and gave him the chance to explain or apologise and instead he chose to have my boyfriend arrested. Not that he was a boyfriend. Not that he is now.

God, I miss him. Just not having his heady scent of grapefruit, sandalwood and musk around me leaves me feeling so lonely and despondent.

I'm waiting for Molly and Alice to meet me for lunch at our favourite local café when Erica comes rushing in. Why does she look so mad? Uh-oh. She's carrying a newspaper.

'Brooke!' She slams the paper down in front of me, taking a seat. 'What the hell is this all about? You sold your story and didn't bloody tell me?'

I roll my eyes. 'Erica, you're not my wife. I don't have to tell you everything.'

'No, I'm your best friend and that should mean something. Why the hell did you ever think this would be a good idea?'

I shrug, ignoring her accusing stare. 'I needed the money to fix my mum's ceiling.'

'Have you seen the article?'

'No, why?'

She flicks it open and points. Staring up at me is the headline 'Local Mayor fathers Illegitimate Daughter', but more shocking than that, there are pictures of me from my Facebook profile. The worst possible photos they could have found.

There's one of me drunk and leaning over the toilet, sticking my middle finger up from last New Year's Eve. One of me squeezing my boobs together, duck pouting my mouth. And the third... the third is me licking a vibrator from an Ann Summers party I went to over three years ago.

'Oh. My. God.'

'Yep,' Erica nods. 'I didn't think you would have willingly handed over those pictures.'

I put my head in my hands. 'This is so mortifying. I mean, I knew people would see it and ask me about it, but I didn't realise they were going to make me out to be some sex-crazed slut.'

'It's okay, hun. The people that know you know the truth.'

I bark out a laugh. 'What?' I grin, 'that I'm a sex crazed slut?'

She bursts out laughing. 'And we love you for it.'

'Brooke!'

I turn, expecting to see Molly and Alice, but only realise half way around that it's a male voice that called me. I find myself facing my dad. His blue icy stare is fixed on me as he walks towards me, his forehead furrowed. Oh shit. What the hell is he doing here?

One look at his reddened cheeks and bloodshot eyes tells me it's to yell at me. My stomach churns with anxiety.

'I'll leave you to it,' Erica says, practically running out of the café.

I go to call him dad, but he doesn't deserve the title. Actually, I have no idea what to call him.

'What are you doing here?' I ask, arms crossed over my chest in what I hope is a confident pose.

I already know the answer before he opens his mouth. Of course, he's read the article. His PR people probably showed it to him before his Weetabix.

'I can't believe you sold your story about me,' he says, his eyes portraying more hurt than anger.

I scoff. 'What, you can't believe I did it? Because you know *so* much about my character from all the years we've known each other? Newsflash, you ran out on my mum the minute she refused to have an abortion.' The journalist lapped that bit up.

He looks around at the people who have turned to stare. 'You don't know the whole story.'

I roll my eyes. 'Which is why maybe you should have had the decency to tell me when I tracked you down. But instead you told me to get lost and had my...' I stop myself saying boyfriend, 'my friend arrested.'

His lips fall into a thin line. 'I told you I wanted to meet up with you away from my family. But you didn't give me a chance before your *friend* was attempting to knock me out.'

I snarl back at him. 'That's because my friend cares more about me than my own father. He couldn't stand how you were treating me.'

My dad looks around at everyone staring. He lowers his voice to a whisper. 'Unlike you, I don't like to make a spectacle of myself.'

God, he's an awful human being.

'Ugh, why did you even come here? Just to shout at me? Well, you've done it, so now you can leave.'

He sighs, rubbing the back of his neck. 'Please, Brooke,' he pleads, 'I just want to talk. Can we go somewhere?'

I'm taken aback by his change of tactics. I have to remember that this guy is in politics. He's used to changing tack in order to get what he wants. Well, if that's true it means he won't leave me alone until I hear him out.

I release my pent-up breath. 'Fine. I'll give you

twenty minutes.'

He nods with a smile. 'After that you don't ever have to see me again if you don't want to.'

I follow him out of the shop wondering just that. Will I want to see him again?

I take "Dad" or the man whose spunk made me as I prefer to refer to him, to a nearby coffee house. It's one of those hipster ones that are ridiculously expensive. He can afford it.

I just hope I don't bump into anyone I know. I don't want to have to introduce him as anything. It would be majorly awkward.

I sit down at a table by the window. He seats himself down across from me and orders a cappuccino from the eager waitress. I order a black coffee. I need pure caffeine right now.

'So, go on then. You wanted to talk,' I offer aggressively. 'So, talk.'

He sighs. 'Brooke, I never intended our first meeting to be like that.'

I scoff. 'I bet you were hoping I'd never sneak out of the woodwork.'

He glares at me. 'Brooke, I don't think you realise that I've been keeping an eye on you for the last couple of years.'

My mouth drops open. Last couple of years? What is he on about?

I shake my head. 'I don't understand.'

'I wanted to find out if you were real.'

'Real? What the hell are you talking about? You've completely lost me.'

The waitress puts our coffees down. I thank her in an effort to get rid of her quickly.

He wraps his hands around it even though it's not cold.

'The thing you have to understand, Brooke, is that me and your mother were never in a proper relationship. Yes, we slept together a few times, but I was always upfront about it not being serious for me. She knew I was only staying with my uncle while my mum was sick.'

I think about that for a minute. I can see that being the truth. Her diary did leave me to believe she was nuts for him.

'But surely when she told you she was pregnant you should have stood up and taken responsibility.'

He scratches his jaw. 'By then your mum had gotten a little obsessed with me.'

'Obsessed with you?' What the hell has this got to do with him telling my mum to abort me?

'I tried to cool it off between us, long before she told

me about you. But she didn't seem to take no as an answer. She started showing up at my uncle's house, calling relentlessly. It was crazy.'

I suppose I know from the diary that she was obsessed with him, but I didn't think it went into stalker territory.

'When she told me she was pregnant, I didn't believe her. I thought it was just another tactic to get me back. So yeah, I told her to get an abortion. I truly didn't believe there was a baby to abort. After that I never heard from her again.'

'And what, you only thought to look me up a few years ago?'

'It wasn't until you were fifteen that your mum contacted me. She'd seen me on a local news programme and looked me up. She wrote me a letter telling me all about you.'

'And yet you didn't try to get in contact?'

Wow, I'm finding it hard to find any redeemable qualities in this man.

'I knew that you were in the middle of your GCSE's then. Me coming into your life would have thrown your world upside down when you needed to buckle down.'

I roll my eyes. 'More like when I bloody needed you. Did you know that I had a miserable childhood? That my mum has always not so secretly resented me? And that

I've had to deal with two horrible half-sisters?'

He swallows, his eyes heavy with some unnamed emotion. 'I did what I thought was right at the time,' he nods seriously, as if trying to convince himself. 'I followed you from afar, seeing you get great results and go off to Brighton University.'

'That's what really hurts. I was SO close the entire time, and you still kept away. That's what hurts the most.'

'Brooke, know that I regret everything. I've got three other children and watching them grow up, its hurt all the more knowing I was never there for you. But by the time I was ready to approach you I was applying for Mayor.'

Ah, now everything is falling into place. He knew an illegitimate daughter would affect him getting elected.

'So, what, you just carried on stalking me because your career was more important to you?'

He looks down at his coffee. 'I have a private investigator that follows you.'

Wait a second. Is this the creep that's been following me around? The one I've been fearing my life over?

'What does he look like?'

He frowns. 'I really don't see how that's relevant.'

I grit my teeth in annoyance. 'It's relevant because

I've been aware of a stalker for the last few months.'

'I don't know,' he shrugs. 'He's medium build with brown hair.'

That's the guy. Rage over takes me.

'So, I've been fearing my own safety all because you had me followed against my will? Do you realise how fucking scared I've been?'

'Language, Brooke,' he admonishes, like he's the father that's been around all of my life. Not the abandoning bastard I've met.

'Don't!' I snap, putting my hand up to stop him. 'Don't try to tell me off like a normal dad. You don't have that right.'

His shoulders curl over his chest. 'I'm sorry, Brooke. I didn't know. He's usually very discreet.'

I roll my eyes. 'Look, none of this even matters. You have your family and I have mine. The friends I chose in life.'

He sits up straighter. 'Well, thanks to you I now have an extremely distraught family.'

'Well, I'm *very* sorry to have inconvenienced your life,' I snarl sarcastically. 'That's all I've ever really been to you, isn't it? An inconvenience.'

'Brooke, you have to understand. My eldest son isn't biologically mine.'

'He isn't?' I ask far too hopefully. The one I made

out with isn't my half-brother? Oh, thank fuck for that! But what, what's that got to do with me? 'And?'

'He's from my wife's previous relationship, but I've raised him as my own. Now after reading today's article he's done the maths and figured that I cheated on his mother. To put him right, we've had to tell him the truth.'

Oops. I mean, I knew I was going to fuck his life up for a bit, but I didn't realise I was going to be unearthing anymore ugly family secrets.

'What about your wife?' I can't help but ask. 'I bet she was furious.'

His face changes the minute I mention her. His eyes soften and a dreamy smile settles on his lips. 'Jenny has always supported me. She's always known about you and my choice to stay away and she's respected that.'

I stop myself from speaking and try to digest all of this for a second. It's too much for my brain right now.

'Look, I have to go.' I stand up and take my bag. 'For what it's worth, I'm sorry I had to do the article.'

Chapter 22

Saturday 9th September

I'm still none the wiser as to how I feel about the whole "Dad" thing. I'm not sure if our conversation proved to me that he wanted to be part of my life—whether his hiring the creepy ass stalker was to show that he cared. Either way, I need to work out myself if I want a relationship with him.

I mean, the fact I have a stepbrother and two half-siblings does sway me. The curious part of me wants to see if we're alike in any way, but the truth is I don't know if I can forgive him for missing out on so much of my life.

He had the stable family I craved so much growing up. Who knows, if I'd have grown up with him maybe I'd have had a completely different childhood.

Maybe I'd have gone to Cambridge instead of Brighton University. Oh, who am I kidding? I'm not a natural brain box like Evelyn. In that boring household,

I would have probably rebelled and ended up a druggie by the time I was fifteen.

I don't have time to obsess over my problems, anyway. I was up early this morning returning my gorgeous silver dress that's still stained to the little boutique. With my best puppy dog eyes I pleaded with them to show mercy. I even cried at one point, but the heartless bitches just rolled their eyes and said they would be offering no money back. I have no idea how I'm going to clear that from my credit card.

I'm helping Erica put the finishing touches to Jack's surprise party. She figures throwing it two weeks after his birthday will make it a real surprise.

People have already started arriving while we're still sticking up banners in our favourite Chinese restaurant's private hire back room. His parents are here welcoming some friends they invited. I still can't look his dad in the eye after the whole underpants thing.

I know any minute now Jack is going to walk in with the boys, on the ruse that they fancy a Chinese. Those boys include Nicholas. I have no idea what it's going to be like between us, but I have to try to not care. I'm here for Erica.

I feel him before I see him. It's like every muscle in my body is suddenly aware of his presence. He's dressed in dark denim jeans with a black shirt. God, he looks utterly fuckable.

'Shit, he's here,' Erica shrieks, spotting a very confused looking Jack. 'Surprise!'

'Surprise!' everyone shouts in a terribly unorganised way.

He grins from ear to ear. 'My God, you guys!'

Nicholas catches my eye and nods, walking towards me as Jack starts thanking everyone. Calm down, Brooke. Do not hyperventilate.

'Hey,' he says with a faint smile.

'Hi,' I offer displaying a weak smile in return. Just being in his presence has me feeling agony over not being able to touch him. 'So... did you speak to your dad?'

'Yeah,' he nods, his eyes clouding over with sadness. 'You were right.'

Damn, I was kind of hoping that I was wrong about his mum.

'I'm so sorry, Nicholas.' I touch his bicep, but he jumps at the contact. It stings. He still can't bear for me to touch him. 'I only did it because I wanted to do something nice for you. It was a desperate attempt at me winning you back. Now I see that it was just another sign we're not meant to be.'

He gazes at me with a probing intensity. 'Don't say that.'

I look down at my shaking hands. 'How can you

not? I bring you nothing but hurt.'

He moves closer and takes my head in his hands.

'Listen to me when I say this, Brooke. You bring me nothing but happiness. Even this with my mum, it's something I needed to find out.'

I force my eyes to the floor. I can't bear looking into those midnight blues knowing he might never forgive me.

'Yeah, but finding out your mum is dead. That must have been devastating.'

He tips my chin with his index finger forcing me to look up at him.

'Obviously it was tough to hear, but in a strange kind of way it's made me finally feel complete.'

I frown. His mum dying has made him feel complete?

'Knowing my mum didn't leave me willingly,' he explains. Okay, that makes more sense. 'My dad showed me her suicide letter. She was in so much pain.' The grief that twists his face makes me cover his hand cupping my chin with mine. 'But one thing she never doubted was how much she loved us both. If anything, she loved us too much. Thought we were better off without her.'

'I'm so sorry.'

He nods, a weak smile on his perfect lips. 'She's at peace now. When I realised that, it was easier for me to imagine her watching over me. Watching us. I know she would have loved you, Brooke. Just like I do.'

I gasp, staring up at him with my mouth open. 'Just like you do what?'

I want to hear him say it. I hold my breath, desperate to hear those three words which hold so much power.

'I love you.'

'You do?' I ask like some pathetic little girl, tears clouding my vision.

'I do,' he nods, stroking my cheek with the back of his fingers. 'And I'm hoping in enough time you'll learn to love me too.'

I laugh, wiping a stray tear from my face. 'I already love you, dickhead.'

He laughs, bringing me in for a strong yet gentle kiss, 'Romantic as ever.'

He breaks away, wrapping me in his arms, my head pressed against his chest. 'This is only the beginning for us. No lies, no secrets, just us.'

'Just us.'

Epilogue

Jessica hugs me goodbye. 'Make sure to call me tomorrow and let me know where Nicholas has taken you.'

I still can't believe I now have a sister I actually get on with. She's like the sister I wish I'd always had, rather than the ugly half-sisters I grew up with. Turns out, having two brothers, she's always been desperate for one too.

Talking of half-sisters, mine have been abandoned by Mum as she decided to take the ceiling repair money and instead go to Tenerife with her current boyfriend. They haven't heard from her since, bar a few postcards. I laughed at first, but it's probably the best thing that could have happened to them. They've had to grow up overnight and even asked for some help in learning how to shop on a budget. We'll never be friends, but one day in the future I hope that we can smile at each other in passing on the street.

My stepbrother, George, nods a goodbye. It's still weird between us. I mean, you don't kiss your stepbrother in the past and get over it that quickly. This isn't Cruel Intentions.

'Have an amazing time,' Dad says, pulling me into an awkward hug. It doesn't matter how much time we spend together, there's still an underlying tension between us. I'm not sure if it'll ever go.

He hasn't done anything so far for me not to trust him. He showed me a box containing birthday cards he'd written to me every year since he'd found out I existed but never had the guts to send. I wish he had.

He'd also started a savings account for me and came to the rescue, paying off my credit card debt from that amazing silver dress. He tells me there's more money in there, but that I won't see it until I buy my first property. Someone has high hopes for me. Has he not seen property prices?

Jenny, my stepmum, pushes him away and squeezes me so tight I almost burst. She's the epitome of a perfect mum. Maternal, caring, overly-nosy. She's got it all. She even insisted we use the unstained material from the silver dress and made me two cushions. Whenever I look at them I remember the way Nicholas' eyes roamed all over me that night; I love them.

'I can't wait to hear about your weekend away.'

Nicholas is taking me somewhere, but he's not telling me where. A surprise weekend somewhere. I just hope it's not Bognor Regis. But as long as there's a hotel room where I can scream as loud as I want I'll be happy.

I look down at the small tattoo on my thumb that matches his. He finally talked me into getting one. I have a Q with a tiny black heart underneath it. It's clear to anyone that sees it that it's a Queen of Hearts symbol from a deck of cards. Nicholas has one on his finger for King of Hearts. It's our way of saying that together we can rule the world.

'Babe,' I call to Nicholas who's playing dominos with my nerdy eighteen-year-old brother, Charles. 'Time to go.'

He smiles at me. I swear, every time he smiles I still get a rush of excitement, my skin turning into goose pimples. I can't believe he's mine. He's made all of this happen. He was the one that encouraged me to give my dad a chance. If I hadn't I wouldn't now have the family unit I always dreamed of when growing up.

And more importantly than that he's shown me how one person can change your life entirely. I've never felt so loved, treasured, adored and respected. He's given me that. I might have given up my single life, but what I've gained in return is an all-consuming love that completes me. I've got Nicholas and I couldn't be happier.

Nan was right. I might be a wild child at heart, but when I choose to love someone it truly knows no bounds.

THE END

Want More?

Don't miss out on the next book in the Babes of Brighton series, Bagging Alice, by signing up for Laura's newsletter - http://eepurl.com/bpR2ar

Acknowledgements

Thank you so much for taking the time to read my book. Reviews mean so much to us indie authors, so I'd really appreciate a quick review on amazon/Goodreads.

Thank you first of all to my family for their continued support. That means me being a sleep deprived zombie mum, unable to form a complete sentence and having to take naps to keep up with my crazy writing hours. It can't be easy living with that!

Thank you to Andrea M Long for her speedy and accurate editing. Her suggestions made the book all it could be. Yummy by Design and DMB Drawings designed this beautiful cover. I just love it!

Thank you to all the readers and bloggers who take time out of their crazy schedules to share my posts and help spread the word. Without you I'd be nothing.

Special thanks to the Indie Author Support Group – you girls are always there for me when I need a sprinting partner or friend for a much needed rant/share/funny message.

Check out Laura's other titles

The Debt & the Doormat Series

The Debt & the Doormat

The Baby & the Bride

Porn Money & Wannabe Mummy

Standalones

Tequila & Tea Bags

Dopey Women

Sex, Snow & Mistletoe

Heath, Cliffs & Wandering Hearts

Adventurous Proposal

Connect with Me

www.laurabarnardbooks.co.uk

www.facebook.com/laurabarnardbooks

https://twitter.com/BarnardLaura

https://www.instagram.com/laurabarnardauthor/

Lightning Source UK Ltd.
Milton Keynes UK
UKOW01f2012071017
310570UK00005B/77/P

9 780995 655430